A Book of Enchantments and Curses

RUTH MANNING-SANDERS

Enchantments are not always evil; sometimes they're even good and benevolent and help someone out of a difficult situation. Curses, on the other hand, are always bad and the person on whom a curse is lain is in for a very hard time . . . .

A BOOK OF
ENCHANTMENTS AND CURSES

Ruth Manning-Sanders

ILLUSTRATED BY
ROBIN JACQUES

A Magnet Book

Other titles by Ruth Manning-Sanders in Magnet books

A BOOK OF MAGIC ANIMALS
A BOOK OF DRAGONS
A BOOK OF MONSTERS
A BOOK OF SORCERERS AND SPELLS
A BOOK OF OGRES AND TROLLS

First published in Great Britain 1976
by Methuen Children's Books Ltd
Magnet Paperback edition first published 1978
by Methuen Children's Books Ltd
11 New Fetter Lane, London EC4P 4EE
Reprinted 1979
Copyright © 1976 Ruth Manning-Sanders
Cover artwork © 1978 Methuen Children's Books Ltd
Printed in Great Britain by
Hazell Watson & Viney Ltd, Aylesbury, Bucks

ISBN 0 416 86610 7

Contents

For permission to retell Black, Red, and Gold *the author wishes to thank Messrs Eugen Diederichs Verlag, Düsseldorf and Köln*

Introduction

One sunny morning I was out walking hand in hand with a very small girl.

'Tell me a story,' said the very small girl.

So I began, 'Once upon a time . . .'

I thought I was getting on nicely, when suddenly the very small girl stopped walking, flung away my hand, stamped her foot, and cried out, '*No*, it wasn't – it wasn't like that!'

'How do you know?' I asked.

'Because I was *there*,' said the very small girl.

Well, after that, of course the story had to go her way, not mine.

Now it would seem that down through the ages so many people of so many different nationalities have, like the small girl, been 'there' – in the magic place where the events told of in these old stories happened. And since of course these many people don't all see with the same eyes, or hear with the same ears, they are each one apt to tell the stories a little differently. But all I need to do here is to tell you from what parts of the world the stories in this book have come, and which stories I should put under the heading of enchantments, and which under the heading of curses.

First the *curses*. *Sarah Winyan*, in the story told by a native of Jamaica, is cursed by her greedy stepmother. The princess in the Sicilian story, *Unfortunate*, is cursed by her evil Destiny. In the story from Pomerania, *The Queen's Ring*, the king is cursed and changed into a frog by a horrid old witch, because he refuses to kiss her. In the German story, *The Curse of the Very Small Man*, the king and the princess are cursed and changed into horses by the very small man out of spite, because he can't get the princess for his wife.

Then the *enchantments*. Well, *A Lying Story* from Pomerania is chock full of enchantments: everything keeps changing into something else, though who works these enchantments we are not told. The Russian story, *Vasilissa* is also full of enchantments. There is Vasilissa's doll, who talks to her and gives her good advice. There are the three horsemen, the white, the red and the black, and the three pairs of hands that appear and disappear at the call of the witch Baba Yaga; there are the skulls that light up at night on the witch's fence, and the skull with its blazing eyes that chases the stepmother and her daughters out of the house. In the Swiss story, *The Enchanted Candle,* it is the candle that works the enchantments (and is also, it seems, itself enchanted). In *The Pick Handle,* an African story, the three girls have learned the art of enchantment from their witch-doctor father, and can change themselves into any shape they will. In the Hungarian story, *The Princess in the Mountain,* a tiny man teaches the musician, Ambrose, two words of enchantment which enable him to change himself into a bear, and back again into a man. Then there is that strange Spanish story, *Black, Red, and Gold,* where the enchantments are the work of three hairs of different colours.

Lastly we come to another Spanish story, *The Knights of the Fish,* in which we find both enchantments and curses. In the beginning of the story the little twin boys are given suits of armour and dappled foals by the enchantments of a fish (and being enchanted, both armour and foals grow as the boys grow). In the end of the story we find the witch of Albatroz working havoc by her curses, until her very rage puts an end to both her curses and herself.

And now about the words themselves – enchantments and curses. If we were to say that a girl was *enchanting*, it would be high praise. It would mean that in her appearance and behaviour she was so attractive as to delight and charm us. But if we were to say that a girl was *enchanted* – that would be a very different matter. It would mean that the poor thing was under a spell, from which we must do all in our power to free her.

The word *curse* is more difficult. We all know what it means, but nobody seems to know just how it came to have that meaning. At any rate, a curse is always a bad thing, never a good. The person upon whom it is laid is in for a very hard time; and it generally takes all the heroic courage and ingenuity of some brave soul to lift it.

1 · Sarah Winyan

A little girl, in a ragged dress, sat under a tree on the edge of a wood. The sun was near to setting, and up in the tree two birds were talking.

Said the first bird, 'Who is that pretty little beggar girl?'

Said the second bird, 'That is Sarah Winyan, but she is no beggar girl. These woods belong to her, and all the land for miles round belongs to her; the grand house you can see over there belongs to her; the very tree we sit in belongs to her.'

Said the first bird, 'Then why does she wear such a ragged little dress, and why does she look so sad?'

Said the second bird, 'Because she has no father and no mother; she has only a cruel old witch of a stepmother, who hates her and wishes her dead.'

Said the first bird, 'Why should anyone hate such a pretty little girl, and wish her dead?'

Said the second bird, 'Because, if Sarah Winyan were dead, all her riches would belong to the stepmother.'

Said the first bird, 'If I were a big strong eagle, I would peck out that cruel stepmother's eyes!'

Said the second bird, 'But you are not a big strong eagle, and neither am I. We are only little fellows, and must leave the world to wag the way it does.'

Then both the birds flew away.

Now the sun set, and Sarah Winyan got up to go back to her grand house. She wiped away some tears with the skirt of her ragged little dress, and began to sing:

> 'Ho-day, poor me, O!
> Poor me, Sarah Winyan, O!

> *They call me beggar, beggar,*
> *They call me Sarah Winyan, O!'*

She was singing that song all the way home. The stepmother was standing at the door of the grand house. She heard Sarah Winyan singing, and she screamed with rage, 'You idle little slut! Didn't I tell you to go into the woods and gather a bundle of sticks for the kitchen fire? Now the fire has gone out, and you come dawdling home empty-handed! You'll get no supper until you bring those sticks. And see that there's plenty,' she shrieked, 'or you'll feel my cane about your shoulders!'

So Sarah Winyan turned back into the woods. And as she was going, she was singing her sad little song:

> 'Ho-day, poor me, O!
> Poor me, Sarah Winyan, O!
> They call me beggar, beggar,
> They call me Sarah Winyan, O!'

The sound of her voice dwindled away into the distance. But the trees and bushes whispered her song to themselves, and the stepmother had sharp ears. 'Sarah Winyan, Sarah Winyan,' she muttered, 'may all the devils in hell fly away with you, Sarah Winyan! Beggar you live, and beggar you shall die!'

And she opened her book of spells, and called up a devil in the shape of a huge shaggy dog.

'Tiger is your name, and tigerish is your nature,' said she to the huge shaggy dog. 'Follow after Sarah Winyan! Follow after that bad girl and tear her to pieces! I will give you a bag of gold. Yes, and I will be your partner when the Lord of Hell calls us to dance the night away on his lofty mountain!'

'You must sign me a contract for that first,' said the big shaggy dog. 'For your ways are slippery as ice, and there's no trusting you.'

So the stepmother wrote out a contract, handing over Sarah Winyan to the devil; and Tiger, that big shaggy dog, took the contract and swallowed it. Then he ran off into the woods after Sarah Winyan.

Now it was growing dark. Sarah Winyan could scarcely see to

gather her sticks. She heard a rushing and a panting and a growling among the bushes. She looked round, and saw two blazing eyes. Oh me, that was one of the stepmother's devils coming after her! Sarah Winyan climbed up into a tree, and crouched there trembling.

Tiger came to stand under the tree. He looked up: he could see Sarah Winyan quite plainly with his blazing eyes. She looked so small, so pitiful, that even his devil's heart was touched.

'Sarah Winyan, Sarah Winyan,' he called, 'come down, come down! You belong to me now; your stepmother has handed you over to me by contract. If you will come down and follow me, I will do you no harm. But if you don't come down, I will pull up this tree by its roots and tear you to pieces!'

Then Sarah Winyan came down from the tree and followed after Tiger through the dark wood. And as she was going, so she was singing her sad little song:

> 'Ho-day, poor me, O!
> Poor Sarah Winyan, O!
> They call me beggar, beggar,
> They call me Sarah Winyan, O!'

Tiger turned round. Sarah Winyan could see his great eyes blazing. 'Stop that song!' he growled. 'I don't like it!'

So Sarah Winyan stopped singing for a little while. Then she began to sing again, but in a very soft whisper. And so she followed and she followed, ever deeper and deeper into the wood.

Meanwhile, back at Sarah Winyan's grand house, the stepmother-witch was gloating. 'Sarah Winyan is dead, is dead!' she was muttering to herself. 'By this time Tiger has torn her to pieces!' And she dressed herself in mourning clothes, and opened her book of spells. 'Let there be a coffin here,' she said, 'and let there be an image of Sarah Winyan lying in it.'

As she said, so it was: there was the coffin, and there was the very image of Sarah Winyan lying in it, all stiff and cold. Then the stepmother put on mourning clothes and tore her hair, and caused a grave to be dug, and called the people together, and had the coffin lowered into the grave. She was screaming and sobbing, and the

people said, 'See how the good stepmother mourns for poor little Sarah Winyan!'

Now amongst the people gathered to the funeral were two young foresters called Aldred and Oti. And as they stood by the grave, Aldred whispered to Oti, 'Brother, there is something wrong here! As we came through the wood just now, surely we heard Sarah Winyan singing. How could she be singing over there in the wood, and at the same time lying here in her coffin? Let us go back now into the wood and seek out the meaning of this mystery.'

So they went back into the wood, carrying their guns. They walked softly, softly. And sure enough, in the very depths of the wood, they heard that sad little whispered song:

> 'Ho-day, poor me, O!
> Poor me, Sarah Winyan, O!
> They call me beggar, beggar,
> They call me Sarah Winyan, O!'

'Brother Aldred,' whispered Oti, 'either that is Sarah Winyan singing, or it is her ghost. But ghost or no, let us follow where it leads.'

So they went on, and they went on. For a time they heard the song, and then they didn't hear it any more. But they saw the faint flickering of a fire. They went towards that flickering, and came to the mouth of a large cavern. They peeped into the cavern. What did they see? They saw a fire burning on a hearth; in front of the fire, they saw Sarah Winyan sitting weeping on a heap of stones, and the devil in the shape of the huge shaggy dog, Tiger, lying fast asleep, with his head on Sarah Winyan's lap.

'Sarah Winyan,' whispered Aldred, 'Sarah Winyan!'

Sarah Winyan looked up. She saw Aldred, she saw Oti. Very, very softly, she reached for a log of wood, slipped the log of wood under Tiger's head, and tiptoed to stand by Oti and Aldred.

Then Oti put a silver bullet into his gun, and took aim at Tiger's head.

Bang! Tiger's head flew into a thousand pieces; and with a yell that echoed round the cavern walls, a little devil leaped out of Tiger's body and fled from the cavern. Now the trees of the wood crashed together, and a great wind roared through them. The little devil rode on the wind, and came to the place where the stepmother, all slobbered up with false tears, was feasting among the guests she had invited to the false funeral. The little devil pounced on the stepmother. He whirled her away in a gale of wind to Hell.

And hand in hand with Aldred and Oti, Sarah Winyan went back to her grand house. In her grand house she lived henceforth in happiness. Aldred and Oti became her dearest friends. They saw to it that no harm came near her. And often and often they heard little Sarah Winyan singing:

> 'Happy, glad me, O!
> Glad me, Sarah Winyan, O!
> They call me lady, lady,
> They call me Lady Winyan, O!'

2 · Unfortunate

There was the good king of Spain, and there was his good queen, and they had seven beautiful young daughters. They lived happily, none more happily, until one day a neighbouring king came with a great army. The king of Spain and his people fought valiantly, but they were defeated: the king of Spain was carried away captive, and the queen and the seven princesses fled into a distant village, where they lived but poorly in a cottage, and tried to earn a little money by doing embroidery and suchlike. But somehow, though their work was beautiful and faultless, nobody seemed to want it, and very often the queen and the princesses had scarcely enough to eat.

Now one summer evening, when the princesses had gone out into the woods to gather wild strawberries, and the queen was alone in the cottage, cooking broth for their supper, an old gipsy woman came knocking at the door, offering some tawdry pieces of lace in exchange for food or money.

'Well, little old grandmother,' said the queen, 'I can give you a bowl of broth and welcome, but of money today I have none at all. I am that unfortunate queen of Spain whose dear husband was carried away prisoner, and now with my seven daughters I live here in poverty. But come in, rest yourself, and if a bowl of broth will content you, that you shall have.'

So the old gipsy woman went in and sat by the fire. She gobbled up her bowl of broth, and then she sat looking into the fire and muttering to herself.

At last she said, 'Queen, for such as I it is given to look into the past and into the future, and to read the causes of things: of the good fortune and the ill fortune that attend us mortals, and of the bringing of the one, and the curing of the other. In your family you have a daughter who is indeed unfortunate; and it is due to her that all this misery has befallen you. She has an evil Destiny. Send that daughter away, and you will win back your king and your kingdom.'

'What,' cried the queen, 'drive away one of my own daughters?'

'Yes, lady, there is no other remedy.'

'But which daughter?' cried the queen. 'They are all so dear, so good – how can I tell which is the one that brings ill fortune?'

'Easily enough,' said the old gipsy woman. 'Tonight, when your daughters sleep in their beds, take a candle and go from one bed to another. Three of the girls will be sleeping on their right sides, with their hands folded together under their chins. Three will be sleeping on their left sides, with their arms under the coverlet. One will be sleeping on her back with her hands crossed on her breast. That is the one you must send away, for on her lies the curse of an evil destiny, and misfortune follows her wherever she goes.'

And so having said, the old gipsy woman went away, leaving the queen in great bewilderment.

Well, by and by, the seven princesses came in. 'We didn't find a single strawberry, not a single one!' they cried. 'Somebody had been in the woods before us and picked them all. Oh, why does everything go wrong for us – why, *why*?'

'Never mind,' said the queen, 'perhaps you will have better luck tomorrow.'

But the princesses said they never had any luck at all. They ate their broth in silence, and then they each one curtsied to their mother, like the well-behaved young princesses they were, and all of them went to bed.

The queen sat for a long time looking into the fire, and thinking of the gipsy woman's words. At last she sighed, lit a candle, and went into the room where the seven princesses lay in seven narrow beds, all sleeping soundly. Tiptoeing from bed to bed, the queen looked down at her beautiful sleeping daughters: three lay on their right sides, with their hands folded under their chins; three lay on their left sides, with their arms under the coverlet; but the seventh, and youngest, lay on her back, with her arms crossed on her breast.

'Oh my darling, my darling, must I send you away?' whispered the queen.

And she wept.

The queen's tears fell on to the hands of the youngest princess; she stirred in her sleep; she woke; she opened her eyes.

'Dearest little mother, why do you weep?'

'Have we not good cause to weep, little daughter? I a queen, and you, my princesses, living like peasants in a tumbledown cottage?'

'But that cannot be the reason,' said the princess, 'or you would have wept long ago. I think something has happened today whilst we were out – tell me what it is!'

'No, no, no!'

But the princess would not listen to 'no'. She bothered and bothered, until at last the queen had to tell her about the gipsy woman and what she had said.

Then the princess threw her arms about the queen's neck, and kissed her many times. 'Go to bed and sleep, dearest little mother,' she said. 'We will think about it in the morning; for the morning is wiser than the evening.'

So the queen went to bed. And no sooner was the queen sleeping than the little princess got up very, very quietly, dressed herself, packed a small bundle of this and that, and stole out of the cottage.

'Goodbye, dear mother, goodbye, dear sisters,' she whispered. 'Now I, Unfortunate, take my leave, that Fortune may come to you again.'

So Unfortunate wandered on her way, and in the morning came to a pleasant house set back in a garden by the side of the road. She peeped in through a window, and saw several ladies at work, some sitting at looms weaving, some spinning, some making lace.

'Perhaps I might find service here,' she thought. And she knocked at the door.

One of the ladies left her loom and opened the door.

'Can I take service here, my lady?' said the princess.

'Oh yes, we need a servant – what is your name?'

'Unfortunate.'

'Well come in, Unfortunate. If you work well, you will find us easy to please.'

So Unfortunate went in, and the lady set her to work, sweeping, cleaning, cooking. She worked with a will, and for a week all went well. And then one day the lady said, 'Unfortunate, my sisters and I are going on a short journey to visit some friends. We shall not return until tomorrow. You bolt the front door and the back door on the inside, and I will lock them on the outside. We can trust you, can we not, Unfortunate, to see that no one gets in to steal the silk and the lace and the cloth we have made?'

'Oh yes, my lady, you can trust me,' said Unfortunate.

So the ladies went away. They locked the doors on the outside, and Unfortunate bolted them on the inside. She spent the day cleaning and polishing till she had everything shining bright. When night came, she went to bed, well satisfied with all her work, and thinking how pleased the ladies would be when they came back. Almost immediately she fell asleep. . . .

But at midnight she woke to hear strange sounds downstairs: muttering and heavy breathing, and the noise of tearing cloth and the snap, snap of rusty scissors. Jumping out of bed and hastily lighting a candle, she ran downstairs. Oh horror, what did she find? A hideous old hag standing amidst a heap of torn lace and cut up cloth – yes, all the fine work of the ladies lay in tattered heaps about the old hag's feet.

'Ha! ha!' laughed the old hag. 'Ha! ha!'

And even as Unfortunate sprang to snatch the scissors from her, the old hag blew out the candle and disappeared. But *how* she went – whether through the locked door, or the barred window – who can tell?

Sobbing bitterly, Unfortunate lit more candles and set about gathering up the tattered cloth and the scraps of cut-up lace. Oh, what would her ladies say when they came back? What *would* they say?

And what *did* they say? 'Ah, you wicked shameless girl, is this our reward for taking you in and being kind to you?' They beat her and drove her from the house: and she wandered on her way, not knowing, or caring, whither she went.

So wandering, she came in the late afternoon to a village; and at

the entrance to the village she saw a little shop that sold bread and vegetables and wine. Having eaten nothing all day, she was very hungry. But she had no money. So, as she stood looking longingly at all the good things to eat in the shop window, the shop woman saw her and came to the door.

'Little one, are you hungry?'

'Oh, I am, I am!'

'Then step in. Things have come to a pretty pass if we can't spare a bite for a poor little soul like you!'

Unfortunate went in, and the shopwoman gave her some bread and cheese and a glass of wine. Then having spoken her thanks most politely, Unfortunate got up to go on her way.

'And where are you going?' asked the shopwoman.

'I . . . I don't know,' said poor Unfortunate.

'But it will soon be dark,' said the shopwoman. 'And the roads are none too safe for young girls. If you care to sleep here at the back of the shop, I can shake down a few sacks for you to lie on.'

So, having again thanked the shopwoman most prettily, Unfortunate lay down on her bed of sacks, and was soon sound asleep, with her hands crossed on her breast.

By and by the shopwoman's husband came in.

'Who is that sleeping on the sacks there?' said he.

'Oh, just a poor little benighted maiden I felt pity for.'

'Well, I hope she may be honest,' said the husband.

And he and his wife went to bed.

All quiet until midnight. Then through the shop window stepped a hideous old hag. The old hag seized up the loaves of bread, tore them into pieces with her clawlike hands, and flung the pieces on the shop floor. Then she knocked over the vegetable baskets, and went striding up and down over the spilled fruit and vegetables until the shop floor was thick with the pulpy mash of everything the baskets had contained. What next? Down into the wine cellar with her, to take the bungs out of all the casks. Now the cellar lay inches thick in a pool of wine and beer. And so, leaving ruin behind her, the old hag stepped out through the window again, and vanished in the darkness.

And all this without a sound.

But when the shopman got up in the morning and saw the wreckage, he snatched up a broom, shook Unfortunate into wakefulness, and beat her. 'You – you – you. . . .' He could scarcely speak for rage. 'Get out, before I kick you out! And if ever I see your face again, I'll. . . . I'll. . . .'

But Unfortunate didn't wait to hear what he would do. She ran out of the shop and out of the village, and away and away and away. She ran out of one kingdom and into another kingdom: and still she ran, until, exhausted, she fell by the roadside in a faint.

So the day passed, the sun set, now it was night; and still Unfortunate lay like one dead at the side of the road. When next morning the rising sun shone on her face, she came to herself, opened her eyes and looked about her. Larks were singing overhead, and near at hand she heard the babbling of a brook. Ah, for a drink of water! She got up and climbed over the fence into a meadow, through which a bright little stream was flowing. Stooping over the stream was a woman, washing clothes.

At the sound of Unfortunate's footsteps, the woman raised her head and looked round. . . . And who should the woman be – ah, who *should* she be – but the old nurse, Dame Francesca, who had dandled Unfortunate on her knees when Unfortunate was a tiny child!

'Nurse, nurse, nurse!'

'My little princess!'

There they were, hugging and kissing each other.

'But what has come to you, my darling, and what are you doing here all alone, and why so pale, and why so ragged?'

Then Unfortunate told Dame Francesca all that had happened. And the Dame, who had brought dinner in a basket, gave Unfortunate to eat and drink.

'I am now laundry woman to the prince of this country,' said Dame Francesca. 'You shall come home with me and live in my cottage until we see better times. For better times will come, my darling, yes, they will come! So now, if you will help me finish my washing, we shall be the quicker done with it, and on our way home

Though to be sure, washing clothes is scarcely work for a princess!'

'I have done every kind of work since I last saw you, dear nurse,' said Unfortunate. And she took up one of the prince's shirts to rinse it in the stream.

Oh me – what happened? The shirt gave a jump and a twist; it jerked itself out of Unfortunate's hands, it floated away down the stream, it caught on the trailing stem of a bramble bush. And when Unfortunate ran to take it off the bush, it had a great tear across the back.

'Yes, I see that you are indeed Unfortunate,' said Dame Francesca. I think you must have an evil Destiny. But never mind, my darling! You shall live with me, and I will wait on you – you shall do no work at all. . . . And I have some thoughts about your Destiny, and how we may set all right.'

So Unfortunate went with Dame Francesca to her cottage and lived there. And as long as she put her hand to no work, all went well. But let her try to help Dame Francesca in any way. . . . If she tried to wash the crockery, it broke under her hand; if she tried to darn Dame Francesca's stockings, the little holes in them grew bigger and bigger; if she tried to sweep out the kitchen, the dust blew back through the door; until at last Dame Francesca said, 'Leave all, leave all! Out with you into the sunshine!'

But no sooner had Unfortunate gone out into the sunshine than great clouds gathered in the sky, and down came the rain.

'Your Destiny is against us,' said Dame Francesca, 'but we'll beat her yet! Now *my* Destiny is a very different kind of person!'

So one day Dame Francesca baked two sweet cakes. She put the cakes in a basket and said to Unfortunate, 'Take these cakes, go and stand on the sea beach, and call my Destiny. Call loud and clear, call three times: "Ah, Destiny of Dame Francesca, ah, Destiny of Dame Francesca, ah, Destiny of Dame Francesca!" At the third call my Destiny will come to you out of the sea. Give her one of these cakes with my greetings, and ask her – very politely, mind – to tell you where *your* Destiny can be found.'

So Unfortunate took the two cakes and went to stand on the sea beach, and called three times, 'Ah, Destiny of Dame Francesca, ah,

Destiny of Dame Francesca, ah, Destiny of Dame Francesca!'

And at the third call a beautiful, shining, smiling lady rose out of the sea.

Then Unfortunate took one of the cakes from the basket, and giving the cake to the beautiful shining lady said, 'Dame Francesca sends you this cake with her compliments. And sweet Destiny of Dame Francesca, would your ladyship do me a great kindness, and direct me to the place where I may find my own Destiny?'

The beautiful shining lady smiled and said, 'Take that narrow mule track over the sandhills and through the thicket. In the midst of the thicket you will find an old hag, sitting under a thorn bush by a well. She is your Destiny. Greet her kindly and offer her a cake. She will be very rude to you, and she will refuse the cake; but lay it at her feet and come away.'

So Unfortunate thanked the lovely lady, and went over the sandhills and through the thicket, and came to where the old hag sat under a thorn bush beside the well. Ah, how hideous that old hag was! How dirty, how blear-eyed, how slobbery, how ragged! Unfortunate trembled at the sight of her and almost ran away. But she pulled herself together, curtsied low, and said, 'My little Destiny, I bring you this cake, if you will be pleased to accept it.'

'Away with it! Away with it!' screamed the old hag. 'I want no gifts of *yours*!' And she spat on the ground, and turned her face away.

So then Unfortunate laid the cake at her feet, and went sadly back to tell Dame Francesca all about it.

Dame Francesca was folding up the prince's laundry. She listened to Unfortunate's tale of woe, and laughed. 'Never say die!' she said. 'We'll win that old hag over yet!'

And she packed the neatly folded laundry into a basket, and hurried off with it to the prince's palace.

'Dame Francesca,' said the prince. 'You are a treasure! Your work for me gets better every day! Here is a little present for you.' And he gave Dame Francesca two gold coins.

What did Dame Francesca do with those two gold coins?

She went into the town and brought an elegant dress, fine under-clothes, a dainty headscarf, a sponge, a cake of sweet-smelling soap, a hair brush and comb, and a bottle of scent. And these things she took home and gave to Unfortunate.

'Now, my darling,' said she, 'off with you again to that old hag, your Destiny; and will she or won't she, strip off her rags, wash her from the top of her head to the soles of her feet, brush, comb, and scent her, and dress her in these new clothes. No doubt she will scream and hit out at you, but be firm, be firm, get on with the work and take no notice of her squawkings. She is but a weak old woman, and you are young and strong. And when she is clean from top to toe, sweetly scented, and dressed as a lady should be dressed, give her this cake and say, "My little Destiny, I, Unfortunate, wish you well. Give me, I pray you, a new name!" '

So Unfortunate took all these things and went over the sandhills to the thicket where her Destiny sat under the hazel bush by the well. She pounced on the old hag, stripped off her clothes, dipped the sponge in the well, and began to wash the dirty old thing from the top of her head to the soles of her feet, whilst the old hag screamed and struggled and called Unfortunate every bad name she could think of. But when Unfortunate, having dried her and sprinkled her with scent, began to dress her in all the fine new clothes, the old hag stopped screaming and chuckled, and every moment she became younger and fairer looking; until, when she was completely dressed, and Unfortunate was combing out her hair, that hair turned from dirty grey to shining gold, and there she was laughing and eating her cake.

Then Unfortunate curtsied low and said, 'My little Destiny, I wish you well. Give me, I pray you, a new name.'

'Ah ha!' chuckled the Destiny. 'Ah ha! That's what you're after, is it? Well then, for the good you have done me, I *will* give you a new name, and your name shall be Fortunata. And here, Fortunata, is a christening present for you,' said she, handing Fortunata a little box.

So happily, happily, Fortunata thanked her Destiny, said goodbye to her, took the little box, and went home to Dame Francesca.

'Now let us see what your Destiny has given you, my pretty,' said Dame Francesca.

And they opened the box.

What was in it? Just a piece of gold braid.

'I don't call that much of a present!' said Dame Francesca.

And she tossed the little box into a cupboard, and bustled off to the palace, to see if the prince had any orders for her.

The prince was dressed in his most splendid uniform, with all his medals and decorations glittering on his coat. But he was walking up and down in a state of distraction. 'Dame Francesca,' he said, flinging out his arm, 'this is disgraceful! There is a piece of braid missing from my sleeve, and in all the town there is no such braid to be bought! Now I am due to review my troops, but how can I face them with my coat in this condition?'

'I think they may not notice it, your highness,' said Dame Francesca.

'*Not notice it!*' cried the prince. '*Not notice it!* What do I care whether they notice it or not? *I* notice it! How can I expect my troops to keep themselves in perfect trim, when I, their commander, appear before them in this slovenly condition?'

'There is a remedy for most things,' said Dame Francesca. And she hurried home, picked up the box that Fortunata's Destiny had given her, and brought it to the prince.

The prince opened the box and looked inside. Yes, it was the very same braid as the braid that was missing from his sleeve.

'My good Dame Francesca,' said the prince, 'I will pay you in gold the weight of this little box and its contents.' And he called for a pair of scales. He put the little box on one scale, and a piece of gold on the other scale. But the gold did not weigh down the little box.

The prince put another piece of gold on top of the first one. But neither did the two pieces of gold weigh down the little box. He put a third piece of gold on the scale, he put a fourth piece, a fifth, a sixth piece: and still the scales did not move. He called for a whole bag of gold and laid it on the scale; but that whole bag of gold did not weigh down the little box.

'Dame Francesca,' cried the prince, 'how is this possible? Can you explain this mystery?'

'I will fetch one who can explain it, my prince,' said Dame Francesca.

And off with her again to her cottage.

'Come, my pretty, come,' she said to Fortunata. 'The prince is asking for you!' And holding Fortunata firmly by the hand, she led her to the prince.

Very pretty, very shy the little princess looked in her shabby clothes. She made the prince an elegant curtsey, and stood silent.

'Who are you?' said the prince. 'And what is your name?'

'I am the youngest daughter of the king of Spain, your majesty,' said the princess 'the king who was taken prisoner, by his enemies. Yesterday I was called Unfortunate; but this morning my Destiny gave me a new name. She said that henceforth I should be called Fortunata.'

'Lovely Fortunata,' said the prince, 'tell me your story.'

So the princess told him everything, and the prince said, 'All this shall now be put right.' He sent for the ladies with whom Fortunata had taken service. And when they stood before him, he said, 'At what price do you reckon the damage that was done to your work on that unhappy night?'

They told him two hundred pieces of gold, and the prince paid them, and said, 'This poor girl whom you have beaten and driven from your door is the daughter of a king. Think of that, and be ashamed! Now away with you!'

So they went shamefaced away, and the prince sent for the shopman whose goods were spoiled; and him also he paid and sent away. And then he summoned his army, and marched off to do battle with the enemy of the king of Spain. In the battle he was victorious; he put the enemy to flight, brought the king of Spain out of prison, and restored his kingdom to him. Then the queen, Fortunata's mother, and Fortunata's six sisters left their poor little cottage, and rejoined the king in his palace.

And after that – well, what after that? Of course Fortunata married the prince. Everyone was happy, including Dame Francesca, who went to live at the palace as head nurse, and bustled about and laughed and sang as she tended the princess Fortunata's pretty babies.

3 · The Enchanted Candle

A handsome boy went looking for work. He walked through the king's city, knocking at this door and that door; but nobody had work for him. So he went out of the city into the country. And it was night, and he was very tired and very hungry. Then, on the edge of a forest, he saw a bright light. He went towards the light, and came to a huge house, with light streaming from every window. He knocked at the door of the huge house: the door opened, and inside was a great hall. And in the hall stood three hideous old women, all dressed alike in long black robes.

'What do you want, handsome boy?' said the first old woman.

'What do you want, handsome boy?' said the second old woman.

And, 'What do you want, handsome boy?' said the third old woman.

'I am seeking for work, if you have any for me,' said the boy. 'And oh, what I want most in the world at this moment is a bite to eat and a drop to drink.'

'You shall have that, handsome boy,' said the first old woman.

'You shall have that, handsome boy,' said the second old woman.

'You shall have that, handsome boy,' said the third old woman.

Then they all three clapped their skinny hands; and there on a table appeared meat and wine and cakes in plenty, and they all sat down to eat. The boy had a plate for himself, and a glass for himself; but the three old women ate out of one huge dish, and drank out of one huge cup. And after they had eaten their fill, they all went to bed.

The boy had a room to himself; but the three old women slept in one bed in a big spare room that had nothing in it but just the bed and a row of lighted candles. Before they got into bed the old women blew out the candles and then lit them again, and then blew them

28

out and lit them again; this they did three times, and got into bed at last with all the candles burning brightly.

The candles were still burning in the morning when the old women called the boy into their room.

'Blow them out, blow out the candles, handsome boy,' said one old woman.

'Blow them out, handsome boy,' said the second old woman.

And 'Blow them out, blow them all out,' said the third old woman.

So the boy went round the room, blowing out one candle after another. And each candle as he blew it out gave a long sigh. But whether it was a sigh of grief or a sigh of pleasure, that the boy couldn't tell.

Then the old women got out of bed and put on their long black robes, and the boy went with them into the great hall, where breakfast was waiting. And again the boy had a plate to himself and a cup to himself; but the old women supped their porridge out of the one great dish, and drank their ale out of the same great beaker.

And after they had eaten their fill, the old women gave the boy a broom and a duster and set him to clean the house. It took him all his time, because the house was very big and very dirty; there were cobwebs and dust everywhere. But he worked hard and he worked well: and the days went by, and the weeks went by, and the years went by, and the handsome boy grew into a handsome lad, none handsomer.

Now every evening after supper the three old women went down into a great cellar, and in the cellar there were hundreds and hundreds of lighted candles. And the old women went round the cellar blowing out the candles and lighting them again. The lad watched them from the top of the cellar steps and wondered why they did it.

'They're crazy, that's what they are,' said the lad to himself. 'And though they feed me well and treat me well, they don't pay me a penny of wages. Maybe it's time I took myself off, and looked for a better place.'

So, as he stood there at the top of the cellar steps, thinking his thoughts, one of the old women looked up and screeched out, 'Hey, handsome lad, we've run out of matches!' And the second old woman looked up and screeched out, 'Hey, handsome lad, our matchboxes are all empty!' And the third old woman looked up and screeched out, 'Hey you, handsome lad, run, run, fetch a matchbox from the bedroom, and bring it down here!'

So the lad ran and fetched a matchbox, and took it down to the cellar. And there were the old women at their games once more, blowing out the candles and lighting them again. And whilst they were busy at one end of the cellar, the lad picked up one of the blown out candles from the other end of the cellar, and put it in his pocket. Why did he do that? Well, I can't tell you; and maybe the lad himself didn't know why. He just took it. And then he forgot about it.

But next morning, when he was dressing, he found the candle in his pocket, and he took it out and lit it. And – what do you think? – the candle up and spoke.

'What do you wish of me?' said the candle.

'Oh!' said the lad, 'Oh! I wish you would bring me into the best tavern in the king's city, and put plenty of money in my pocket.'

And – bless me! – all in a breath, there was the lad seated in a fine room in a great tavern in the king's city, with the blown out candle and the matchbox still in his hand, and his pockets fair bulging with gold coins.

'Oh, ho!' said the lad. 'Oh ho! Now we are beginning to learn things!' And he struck a match and lit the candle again.

'What do you wish of me?' said the candle.

'A suit of clothes fit for a prince,' said the lad. 'Myself wearing that suit, and myself with the looks and airs and manners of a prince, and my pockets always full of gold coins.'

No sooner said than done. The lad went to stand before a looking glass and laughed. 'A prince you are truly,' said he to his image in the glass. 'Good morning to you, my prince!' said he. And he bowed to his image in the glass. 'Prince of Fairland we will call you, my handsome,' said he. 'And now out with you to take a stroll through the city.'

Then he blew out the candle, put it, with the matchbox, safely into his pocket, and off with him, proud as a peacock, to walk about the city.

Well, he hadn't been walking long when there came a coach driving down the street, and in the coach sat the king's daughter, a very lovely little princess. The princess looked at the lad and smiled. The lad looked at the princess, and his heart fairly thumped, and his head fairly whirled, for surely she was the most beautiful maiden that ever the sun shone on.

'Oh!' said he. 'Oh!' And he turned and went straight back to his room in the tavern.

He took the candle out of his pocket and lit it.

'What do you wish of me?' said the candle.

'Bring me the princess here, and hurry, hurry!' said the lad.

And there she was, standing in the room and smiling at him.

'I don't know how I got here,' said the princess.

'Never mind how you got here, since here you are,' said the lad.

'But who are you?' said the princess.

'The Prince of Fairland, at your service,' said the lad.

'And what do you want of me, Prince of Fairland?' said the princess.

'Just to stay by my side a while, and let me tell you how beautiful you are,' said the lad.

'You're not bad looking yourself,' said the princess.

And she laughed, and sat down beside him.

So they chatted a while. And by and by they were holding hands. And next the lad had the princess in his arms. And next they were hugging and kissing. And next they were planning to get married, and promising to be true to each other for ever and ever.

'But I don't know what my papa will say,' said the princess. 'He has already betrothed me to a horrid old duke. But I won't, I won't, I *won't* have any husband but you, my prince!'

And she stamped her pretty little foot and looked quite fierce.

Then she went home, and told the king that she wasn't going to marry the horrid old duke.

'And why not?' said the king with a scowl.

'Because I love someone else,' said the princess.

'And who may this someone else be?' said the king, very angry.

'The handsomest lad in the world, the Prince of Fairland,' said the princess.

'I'll give him handsome lad!' cried the king. 'There is no such place as Fairland! I won't have you going about picking up with any good-for-nothing beggar that takes your fancy!'

And he locked the princess up in her room, where she sat and cried. Then he sent soldiers to fetch the lad, and had him put in prison, and chained to an iron ring.

But the lad took the candle out of his pocket and lit it.

'What do you wish of me?' said the candle.

'I want you to set me free,' said the lad, 'and take me back to the tavern. And I want the king to be fastened up here in my place.'

Said and done. The lad was back in the tavern, and the king was in the dungeon, chained to the iron ring.

The king was shouting and cursing, and calling to his soldiers to set him free. The soldiers came running; they couldn't undo the chain. The king sent for blacksmiths; they came running with hammers and chisels and saws; but no, they couldn't undo the chain. All that happened was that the chain grew tighter and tighter round the king's body, until he could scarcely breathe.

So at last he panted out, 'Fetch the lad here, fetch the lad!'

Well, they fetched the lad. He didn't hurry. He came strolling into the dungeon. And if he wasn't a prince, he had the airs of one.

'Good morning, my lord king,' said he. 'What can I do for you this morning?'

'Blackguard, set me free!' cried the king.

'That is not the way to address a prince,' said the lad.

And he turned to go out of the dungeon.

'No, no, no!' cried the king. 'Don't go! I don't care who you are – you may be the devil, for all I know! But set me free, and I will give you anything you ask!'

'The princess to be my wife?' said the lad.

'Yes, yes,' cried the king. 'My daughter to be your wife!'

'Is that a promise?' said the lad.

'Yes, it is a promise,' sobbed the king. But in his heart he cursed the lad, and said to himself, 'Yes, he shall marry my daughter . . . but he shall not live another hour after the wedding!'

Then the lad went back to the tavern and lit the candle.

And the candle said, 'What do you wish of me?'

'I wish you to set the king free from his bonds,' said the lad. 'And I wish you to bring me here princely wedding raiment. And I wish you to arrange all things fitting for my marriage with the princess. And perhaps if you were to bring me a sharp-cutting sword it would not come amiss. For I have a feeling I may need it.'

Then all was done as the lad ordered. He held his wedding with the princess, and it was a very grand one. The lad was happy, the princess was happy; they feasted and made merry with the wedding guests. But the king, the princess's father, was scowling. And the queen, the princess's mother, was scowling. And the king whispered to the queen, 'The imposter shall not live another day!'

'He shall not live even another night,' whispered the queen.

So, when the feast was over and the guests had gone, the lad went up to the splendid room that had been prepared for him and his bride. And there he took the candle out of his pocket, set it in a saucer on the table and lit it.

The candle said, 'What do you wish of me?'

'I wish you to tell me whether my princess and I are going to be happy,' said the lad.

'No, that you are not!' said the candle. 'Because the king and queen are going to kill you. He has a sword, and she has a dagger. They are hiding under the bed at this very moment.'

The lad snatched up his own sword from the table, and looked under the bed. Sure enough, there was the king, and there was the queen, he with a sword, she with a dagger.

'Bring them out,' said the lad to the candle.

And willy nilly, out crawled the king, and out crawled the queen.

'Just a little joke,' said the king, looking very silly.

'Yes, just a little joke,' said the queen, looking equally silly.

'Your joke does not amuse me,' said the lad. 'Candle, take these jokers away.'

'Where shall I take them?' asked the candle.

'To the kingdom of Fairland,' said the lad with a laugh. 'And there let them reign forever and a day.'

In a moment king, queen and candle vanished. And in another moment there was the candle back again in its saucer still brightly burning.

'Are they gone for good and all?' said the lad.

'Yes, they are gone for good and all,' said the candle.

'Then I ask you again,' said the lad, 'are my princess and I going to be happy?'

'Yes,' said the candle, 'you will both be happy: she as queen and you as king. Now you will need me no longer. And after all I have done for you, I think you should do one little thing for me.'

'And what little thing is that, my candle?' said the lad.

'Just to let me burn down,' said the candle. 'I am weary of this game of light and darkness, light and darkness. I want an end to it.'

'Have it your own way, my candle,' said the lad. 'Now I will go and fetch my bride.'

So he left the candle burning and went from the room. And when he came back, hand in hand with the princess, there was no light in the room, except the moonlight that shone in through the window. And on the table, in the saucer where the candle had burned, there was only a little pool of wax.

4 · The Queen's Ring

A queen went out to walk in the meadows. The queen was very beautiful, but she was also very sad: because many months ago the king, her dear husband, had gone away to the wars; and in all these months the queen had no news of him.

'But he cannot be dead,' said the queen to herself. 'If he were dead I should surely know it.'

So, after she had wandered here and there, the queen sat down by a well to rest. She often came to the well, because it was at this spot that the king had given her his last kiss before he rode away. And it was here that he had put on her finger a diamond ring, and said, 'Keep this ring carefully, look at it often, and when you look at it think of how much I love you!'

Now, as she sat by the well, the queen took the ring from her finger and laid it against her cheek. 'Dear ring,' said she, 'dear ring, night and day I think of him who gave you to me! Dear ring, tell me, oh tell me where he is!'

Then, oh me, what happened? The ring slipped from the queen's hand and fell into the well.

'My ring, my ring!' cried the queen, leaning over the water. The well was deep, and the ring had sunk to the very bottom of it – what was she to do? She leaned over the water, she couldn't even see the ring, no, not the least sparkle of it. 'My ring, my ring!' She wept and wept.

Then out of the well clambered a big green frog.

'Why do you weep, beautiful queen?' said the frog.

'My ring, my ring!' cried the queen. 'I have dropped it into the well, and I cannot, cannot get it again!'

'But surely the queen is rich – she can buy another ring?' said the frog.

'No, no, *no*!' cried the queen. 'Not another ring like this, for this ring my dear husband gave to me before he went away.'

'And do you value it so much because of that?' said the frog.

'I value it above everything else in the world!' cried the queen.

'Well then,' said the frog, 'if you will give me what I ask, I will dive back into the well and bring up your ring.'

'I will give you anything you ask,' said the queen.

'Is that a promise?' said the frog.

'That is a promise,' said the queen.

So the frog dived back into the well, and soon came up again, holding the ring in one of its webbed hands.

How the ring sparkled! How the queen laughed, though the tears were still on her cheeks. 'Oh, thank you, thank you, dear frog,' she said. 'And now, what shall I give you?'

'Just a kiss on my mouth,' said the frog.

'Oh!' said the queen. 'Oh, I cannot give you that!'

'Why not?' said the frog.

'Because,' said the queen, 'you are . . .' she was going to say, 'so ugly and slimy', but no, that would be too ungrateful. So she said. 'A queen can kiss no one but the king her husband.'

'Then I will put the ring back where I found it,' said the frog. And he was about to jump into the water again, when the queen cried out, 'No, no, I will kiss you, I will kiss you!'

And she picked up the frog, shut her eyes, and kissed its cold gaping mouth. . . .

'Now open your eyes, my dearest!' said a laughing voice. Whose voice? The voice of the king her husband! Yes, the frog had vanished, and there in its place stood the king, her husband, stooping to take her in his arms.

And this is the tale he told her: 'After the war was over, my darling, I was riding home at the head of our victorious troops when we lost our way in a thick mist. My men rode this way and that way, searching for the road. I could hear their voices and the sound of their horses' hoofs growing fainter and fainter; and when the mist lifted it was night, and I found myself alone, in front of a small

house in a deep forest. I got off my horse and went into the house to ask for a night's lodging; and in the house I found a beautiful damsel seated on an ivory stool before a golden spinning wheel, spinning silver thread.

'"What will you give me in return for a night's lodging?" said the beautiful damsel.

'"Whatever you ask," said I, "and whatever I can."

'"You can easily give me what I ask," said the beautiful damsel. "All I ask is a kiss."

'"But that is something I cannot give," said I. "I kiss no one but my own dear queen."

'Then the damsel sprang up from her ivory stool. But she was no longer beautiful. She was indeed a hideous witch. "You call yourself a king!" she screamed, "you are nothing but a cold-blooded frog!" And she struck me with her distaff. Then my limbs dwindled, and my body shrank, my mouth grew wide, my eyes goggled. Yes, she had turned me into a frog.

'"A frog you are, and a frog you shall remain, until some lovely woman of her own free will kisses you on your gaping mouth!" she shrieked. And she took me up by one leg and flung me out through the door.

'"I kiss no one but my own dear queen," I said again, as I crept away into the forest.

'Then began my weary journey home. Days and nights, days and nights went by. I passed through many kingdoms. Journeying by day, resting by night in some hidden corner of great palaces or peasants' cottages, I saw many lovely women, both high-born queens and princesses, and lowly village maidens. Perhaps one of them would have taken pity on me and kissed me had I asked them. "But no," I told myself. "I never have kissed any woman but my own dear queen, and I never will kiss any woman but my own dear queen. And if it takes me the rest of my life, I will come at last to where she waits for me."

'And so, my darling, the poor little frog journeyed on and on, through great cities, and over wide moors, through rushing rivers, and dense forests, on and on and on, until, at last, that poor little frog came home into his own kingdom. And the rest you know, my darling.'

Then the king put the ring back on the queen's finger, and hand in hand they returned to their palace, where they lived happily ever after.

5 · The Curse of
the Very Small Man

A prince sat by the side of the road in a desolate country. And there came walking up to him a very small man.

'Are you happy?' said the very small man.

'*No!*' said the prince.

'Why aren't you happy?' said the very small man.

And the prince answered, 'My witch of a stepmother has driven me out of my kingdom. Here I sit by the roadside in a strange land, hungry and thirsty, without a drop to drink or a crust to put in my mouth, and you ask me *am I happy!*'

'Well,' said the very small man, 'here's a flask of wine and a currant bun for you.'

So the prince swallowed down the wine and ate up the currant bun. Now he felt better.

'Thank you indeed!' said he.

'Now,' said the very small man, 'you shall come home with me. I can give you work; and if you are willing and obedient, all will go well.'

'I can certainly be obedient, and I expect I shall be willing,' said the prince.

And he got up and went with the very small man.

The very small man took him to a very large castle, in which there were many fine rooms and beautiful objects, but not a living soul except the prince himself and the very small man – though there must have been some invisible presences there, because, when the very small man clapped his hands and said, 'Dinner for two!' there was a sumptuous meal set out on a silver table. And the prince and the very small man sat down to eat.

After they had eaten, the very small man took the prince into a library, stacked from floor to ceiling with shelves full of books.

'You may amuse yourself and improve your knowledge in your spare time with these books,' said the very small man. 'But there is just one book, the one in the red and gold binding on the second shelf in the corner there, that you may not open, much less read. For should you open and read it, you will come into great misfortune. And don't you get the idea into your head that you can disobey me in anything, for I have my own ways and means of knowing what you do.'

So, after the very small man had shown the prince all over the castle, he took him out into a stable. In the stable were two handsome animals, a silver-grey mare and a raven-black stallion.

'You will groom these two every morning until their coats shine,' said the very small man. 'And you will feed them twice a day. To the grey mare you will give two tankards of wine to drink, and plenty of good bread to eat. To the black stallion you will give, twice a day, a bucket of oats and a pailful of water. That is all the work I require of you. In your leisure hours you may saddle the black stallion and ride him where you will, about the meadows and through the forest. But you must never ride the grey mare, or let her out of the stable, and you must put the stallion back in his stall before dusk. And never, never must you go into the stable with a light. Now is it clear what your duties are, and what you may do, and what you may not do?'

'Yes, it is quite clear,' said the prince. 'My duty is to look after the two horses. My free time I may spend reading in the library or out riding. I may ride the black stallion by day, but the grey mare not at all. I must not open the book in the red and gold binding on the second shelf in the corner of the library; I must never bring the grey mare out of the stable, and I must never go into the stable with a light.'

'Good!' said the very small man. 'As for myself, I travel frequently about the country; but when I am not here, you have only to clap your hands and ask for what you want – be it food, raiment, lights, music, or anything else, and what you ask will be given you. Be obedient, be diligent, and fortune will smile on you. But woe betide you if you dare to disobey!'

Then the very small man went away, and the prince set to work to groom the two horses. They seemed pleased to have him there, and they whinnied gently and nuzzled him with their soft noses. So, when he had groomed and fed them, the prince went back into the castle, and amused himself for some time by looking through the books in the library. And after that he saddled and bridled the black stallion, and went for a ride about the palace grounds and into the forest.

Before dusk he was back again in the stable, feeding and bedding down the mare and the stallion; and then came a good supper with the very small man, and so to his bed in a magnificent room, where unseen hands helped him to undress, and clothed him in a silken sleeping robe.

'Not a bad life this!' said the prince with a yawn, as he curled up under the bedclothes.

So life went on from day to day, the prince having no company but the two horses and the very small man, who appeared and disappeared at all sorts of odd moments, and rubbed his skinny hands together, and chuckled, and told the prince he was doing well, and that he was pleased with him. 'Go on in the way you are going,' said the very small man, 'and I will make your fortune for you. Any complaints?'

'None,' said the prince. But he thought, 'I could do with some company other than you.'

'Oh, so you could, could you?' said the very small man. 'Don't you have too many thoughts of that kind! Because I can read you as easily as you can read the simplest book in my library.'

'Indeed and I beg your pardon,' said the prince. 'But you must remember I am but young.'

'You are growing older every day,' said the very small man. '*And* wiser, I should hope! Now listen to me. Tomorrow I am setting out on a journey. I shall be away for some time. But don't you get it

43

into your head that I shan't know what you are doing here. Distance makes no difference to me.'

'Then I think, sir, you must be a magician?' said the prince.

'Perhaps, perhaps,' said the very small man. 'Now off to bed with you. I shall be gone before you wake in the morning.'

And, sure enough, when the prince got up next day, the very small man was nowhere to be seen.

Before he sat down to breakfast, the prince went to the stable to feed and groom the two horses. And they greeted him as usual with affectionate whinnies and nuzzlings. 'Dear creatures,' said the prince, 'if it wasn't for you two, my life here would be unbearable! Do you understand what I am saying? Yes, I believe you do! We are surrounded by mystery all three of us. We will go for a gallop after breakfast, my Black. And you, dear Grey, how I wish I could take you with us! But I may not, no, I may not, for I believe I am a doomed man if I dare to disobey.'

Surrounded by mystery: that feeling was with the prince all day; and in the evening he could not rest, so he went out to stroll about the castle grounds. The moon had risen, there was a little breeze, and the shadows of tree branches and bushes wavered in the moonlight. The prince was making his way down a wooded glade, when, to his utter astonishment, he saw two figures walking arm in arm down the glade ahead of him. One figure was that of a stalwart man in a long black robe, the other that of a young woman in a silver-grey mantle. The prince could hear the low murmur of their voices: the voice of the young woman broken by sobs; the voice of the man, gentle and would-be comforting. But what either of them was saying, he could not hear.

Who could these two people be, and why were they here where no one came? Greatly startled, and somewhat scared, the prince turned and went back into the castle. Roaming from silent room to silent room, puzzling over what he had seen, the prince at last settled down in the library, and took down book after book, attempting to read and compose his mind. But the vision of those two figures came between him and his reading, and he cast book after book aside. Then his eyes fell upon the book in the red and gold binding on the second shelf in the corner – the book he had been forbidden to read. And distractedly he took down the book and opened it.

Ah, he soon found why he had been forbidden to read it, for the story was all there: the story of a king and his daughter to whom the castle belonged, and whom the small, the very small man had enchanted, snatching their castle and their lands from them, and turning them into two horses, the king into a black stallion, and the princess into a grey mare. The book also told how they could be freed from enchantment, and the prince was promising himself that he would quickly set about the task, when he heard a growling sound at his elbow. . . . And behold, there was the very small man himself standing at his side.

'Wretch, sneak, imbecile!' growled the very small man. 'What are you about? I have saved you from starvation, I have given you food and lodging, I have pampered you as a son, and this is the way you show your gratitude!'

And he gave the prince a kick that sent him flying through the library door. He gave the prince another kick and sent him flying through the great door of the castle. 'Now you may go and feed swine,' he yelled; 'it is all you are fit for!'

And the prince, as he scrambled to his feet on the castle terrace, heard the great door slammed and bolted behind him.

What to do now? He wandered off into the night. The moon went down, and by and by it was dawn. The prince wandered on through a silent country of forests and plains, where he met no one. He wandered for days, weary, hungry, footsore, feeding on roots and berries, cupping up water from sullen streams to quench his thirst.

So he wandered for a week, and then came in sight of a village.

To this village he hastened. It was market day, and the peasants were gathered in the village square, buying and selling.

'Has anyone of you need of a labourer?' asked the prince of the peasants.

Yes, one of them had need of a swineherd, and he engaged the prince for his bed and board and a few coppers a week.

So, next morning, there is our prince setting out with a herd of

swine for some flat waste ground under a great mountain. And whilst the pigs snuffled and grunted and rooted among bushes and grass, the prince sat on a hummock and looked about him, and thought of all he had read in the forbidden book in the very small man's library. In that book he had read of the great bird Gryff, and of a white egg in the bird's stomach, and of what would happen could anyone get hold of that egg and break it on the very small man's head. And as he so sat and thought, the prince heard a whizzing and a roaring in the air, and looking up he saw the great bird Gryff itself hovering above him.

The great bird Gryff made a swoop or two as if he would snatch up one of the pigs, but a rock from the prince's strong right arm came hurtling up at him, so the bird flew off and alighted on the mountain; and there he perched, turning his head from side to side, with the sun lighting up the tuft of green feathers on his head.

In the evening, after the prince had driven the herd of pigs back to their sties, he told the peasant about the great bird Gryff.

'Ah, the villain,' said the peasant, 'that bird has stolen many a pig from me. So don't you drive them near the mountain.'

'The bird won't steal any pigs from me,' said the prince, 'drive them where I will.'

'Just you see that he doesn't,' said the peasant, 'if you don't want to feel my stick across your back, and find yourself kicked from my door. But come now, eat your supper and get to your bed, for it's early to bed and early to rise with the likes of us.'

'Well, well,' said the prince to himself, 'little did I think, before my stepmother snatched my kingdom from me, that I should live to be ordered about by a peasant in a smock. But as we live, so we learn!'

Next morning the prince was up at dawn; he got a bowl of porridge and a curt word or two from the peasant, and then set out once more, driving the herd of pigs before him. Where did he drive them? Straight to the foot of the mountain, for he was thinking of what he had read in the book with the red and gold binding, and he knew what he was going to do.

So whilst the pigs grunted and rooted among the bushes and grass, the prince sat on a rock, fingering a dagger which he carried at his belt, and watching the sky, and waiting.

Towards midday the likeness of a great dark cloud passed between the prince and the sun; and, looking up, he saw the great bird Gryff hovering over his head. The great bird hovered for a moment over the herd, then with a sudden swoop he seized up one of the pigs in his talons. But the prince gave a spring, snatched the pig from Gryff's talons, and tore three feathers from the bird's breast. One feather he took in his mouth, and the other two he put behind his ears. Now he could fly.

Up and up went the great bird Gryff, and up flew the prince after him. And, as they reached thin air the great bird tired, giving the prince his chance. He stuck his dagger up into the bird's throat, and the bird fell out of the sky – dead. Then quickly the prince sank down to earth, cut open the Gryff's stomach, and took from it a big white egg. So, with the egg in his pocket, the prince gathered his pigs and drove them back to the peasant's cottage.

The peasant, who was digging up potatoes in his garden, began to shout and scold, demanding to know why the prince had brought the herd back so early in the day. But his scolding ended in a gasp of astonishment, as the prince gave a leap into the air, and flew off into the western sky.

The prince flew on; he came to the very small man's castle, and there he perched in a linden tree near the stables, and waited for dusk. And at dusk the stable door opened, and out stepped the stalwart man in the black robe, and the young woman in the silver grey dress, followed by the very small man.

The prince took the big white egg from his pocket, and watched and waited. . . . Now the three figures were approaching the linden tree. The very small man was ranting and raving, the young woman was weeping, the stalwart man was speaking in a low voice, seeking to comfort her.

'This is your last chance!' screeched the very small man. 'If I have any more of your disobedience and miserable complaints, I'll change you both into *rats!* And you can gnaw your way out of the stable and pick up your own garbage for all I. . . .'

Smack! The great Gryff's egg dropped from the prince's hands and broke over the head of the very small man.

Then arose a furious storm; lightning flashed, thunder roared, the earth heaved, the linden tree bowed and shook. The prince clung to a branch of the tree; he could see nothing but the flashes of lightning, hear nothing but the peal after peal of thunder.

'This is the end of me, and of the world!' he thought, as the tree fell over with a crash. . . .

But it was not the end of the prince, or of the world: only the end of the very small man, who lay dead under the fallen tree. Now the prince, scrambling to his feet, saw standing by his side a stately king in a golden crown, and a beautiful young princess, wearing a silver grey dress sparkling with diamonds. And now out of the castle came running a crowd of people, lords in waiting and ladies in waiting, courtiers, pages, men servants and women servants, all shouting for joy and hailing the prince as their deliverer.

'Yes, you are indeed our deliverer,' said the king with the golden crown. 'You have freed us all from the spells of the evil little dwarf, who, because I refused to give him the princess, my daughter, in marriage, changed me into a black stallion, the princess into a grey mare, and my people into invisible ghosts. But now all is well. You, prince, shall be my heir, and if you and the princess are willing, we will hold a merry wedding. What say you, my children?'

'Oh *yes*!' said the princess.

And 'Oh *yes*!' said the prince. 'And though I once had a kingdom of my own, which my stepmother stole from me – well, she can keep it. I have no wish to go back and do battle with her.'

So the prince and the princess were married, amid great rejoicings. And king, prince, and princess lived happily ever after.

6 · A Lying Story

Once upon a time a young blacksmith put his hammer and some nails and a loaf of bread into a knapsack, and set out to see the world.

Well, he hadn't travelled far when he met a tailor.

'Where may you be going?' says one to the other.

'On my travels. And you?'

'On my travels, also.'

'Well then, let us go along together.'

Agreed. So they went along together, and they came into a great forest. And in the forest they met a man dressed in green with a gun upon his shoulder.

'Good day! Good day! You are doubtless a hunter?'

'That is plain to see. And you two, of what trades are you?'

'I am a blacksmith and he is a tailor. And we are off to foreign parts to seek our fortunes.'

The hunter said, 'May I come along with you?'

'Yes, come!'

So the three of them walked along, and they walked along. They were walking all day through that forest, but not one of them knew where they were going. And now it was night.

Where to sleep? Then they saw a little light glimmering through the trees, and they went towards the light. Now they were standing in front of a little house.

'Anyone at home?'

No answer.

'May we come in?'

No answer.

So they went into the little house, and found a room with three beds in it, and a fire burning in the hearth. They found two barrels also, one full of salt meat, the other filled with beer. And on the wall hung three rifles, each with its bag of shot and powder horn.

'Ha ha! Ho ho! This is the place for us!' said the smith.

'Yes, the very place for us!' said the other two.

So they warmed themselves at the fire, took a joint of meat from one barrel and cooked it, drew some beer from the other barrel, had a good meal, and slept off their weariness in the soft beds.

Well, they thought they might as well stay a while in the little house. So, next morning, after they had made a breakfast of meat and beer, they decided that two of them should go out into the forest and shoot game, and the third should stay behind and cook the dinner. They drew lots as to which should stay, and the lot fell on the tailor.

The tailor was quite glad to stay behind: he wasn't much of a shot, but he was handy about the house. So he tidied up the room, and got a good fire going. He found some turnips and carrots on a shelf, cut them up into tidy pieces, took some meat out of the barrel, and hung up a cauldron full of water over the fire to boil. He was just going to put everything into the cauldron to make a stew, when the door flew open, and in strutted a tiny, tiny mannikin, with a long, long beard.

'Little tailor, little tailor,' said the tiny, tiny mannikin, 'now I shall blow out your fire for you!'

'You'll do no such thing, Mr. Impertinence!' cried the tailor. 'You leave that fire alone, and be off with you!'

And he made a jump to push the mannikin out of the house. But the mannikin made a jump to the stove. *Huff puff!* See there – the fire was out, and the mannikin had disappeared.

Could the tailor light that fire again? No, he couldn't. Paper wouldn't burn, sticks wouldn't light, coal remained black and sullen. The tailor gave up trying in the end; and when his two comrades came back tired and hungry, well – no fire, no dinner!

'*I* can't help it,' said the tailor sulkily.

And he told them what had happened.

But they just laughed at him. 'What, a mannikin, six inches high! Is it likely? Come now, confess, you fell asleep and dreamed it all.'

But they weren't too pleased when they had to dine on cold meat out of the barrel.

Next morning it fell to the hunter's lot to stay at home and cook the dinner. 'And no impudent mannikin shall blow out *my* fire!' said he.

The same thing happened that day as had happened the day before. No sooner had the hunter got a good fire going than the door flew open, and in came the mannikin with the long, long beard.

'Hunter, ah little hunter, now I shall blow out your fire for you!' cried the mannikin, skipping over to the hearth.

And *huff puff* – the fire was out. The mannikin vanished. And the hunter spent the rest of the day struggling with paper that wouldn't burn, sticks that wouldn't light, and coal that remained black and sullen.

'I thought as much!' said the tailor, when he and the blacksmith came home in the evening, tired and hungry.

But the blacksmith said, '*I* shall stay home tomorrow, my friends, and no wretched little mannikin is going to get the better of *me!* Just let him try!'

Well, next morning, as soon as they'd had breakfast, the tailor and the hunter took their rifles and went off into the forest. And, as soon as they'd gone, the blacksmith took a hammer and some nails out of his knapsack, and laid them on a bench by the stove. Then he lit the fire. And sure enough, just as the fire was burning merrily, the door flew open, and in hopped the mannikin.

'Smith, ha, little smith!' cried the mannikin. 'Now I shall blow out your fire for you!' And, *hipperty hop*, over with him to the stove.

But the smith seized up the hammer in his right hand, and a long nail in his left hand, and with one blow he struck the nail through the mannikin's ear, and nailed him fast to the wall.

And there the mannikin hung all day, whimpering and squealing, and twisting himself this way and that way, whilst the blacksmith kept up a merry fire, skinned and roasted two hares, and cooked a pan full of carrots and turnips.

'What did I tell you?' said he, when the tailor and the hunter came back. 'No little tom-tit-tot of a mannikin gets the better of *me!*'

So they all sat down to eat. And when they had eaten their fill, and were ready for bed, they thought about getting the mannikin away from the wall.

'We don't want him squealing at us all night,' said the blacksmith. 'We best put him outside.'

And he stepped over to pull the nail out of the mannikin's ear.

But the mannikin gave a howl, and tore himself loose. And – would you believe it? – he turned from a tiny mannikin into a huge green giant of a man, and the nail in his ear turned into a long sword that hung by his side.

There stood that green giant, scowling fiercely, and never saying a word.

The tailor and the hunter and the blacksmith stood still also, and neither did they say a word, for very terror. But by and by they began softly, very softly, to tiptoe to the door, thinking to get away into the forest. Then the door flew open and in stepped a green giant of a woman, barring their way. The smith swung his hammer and struck a nail through the giant woman's head, nailing her to the door post. But even as he thought to get past her and run out, she wrenched herself free and turned into a great black bear that opened its mouth wider than the door itself, as if to swallow them all.

'Shoot! Shoot!' cried the smith to the hunter.

The hunter took aim and shot the bear through the heart, so that it sank to the floor. But the dead bear turned into an immense horse, and in a flash the giant by the stove swung himself on to the horse's back, and made to ride out through the door. But both horse and giant were in such a hurry to get outside that the giant forgot to duck his head, and – *smack* – he struck his head against the lintel, and the head rolled back into the room. Then the horse and the headless rider galloped off full tilt into the forest, and were never seen again.

'Now perhaps we can go to our beds and sleep in peace!' said the blacksmith. 'But first to get rid of this object!' And he picked up the head by its hair and flung it outside the house.

Heaven help us! The head turned itself into a barrel organ; and the tailor, who was feeling a bit crazy, what with one thing and another, seized the handle of the barrel organ and began to play. Yes, it played as a barrel organ should; it played tune after tune, and it was a pleasure to hear it.

'We'll take the barrel organ with us on our travels,' said the blacksmith. 'But we won't stay in this peculiar house much longer. I think we had better set off first thing in the morning, before any more strange things happen. What do you say, my friends?'

'Oh yes, first thing in the morning, before we all go mad!' cried the tailor and the hunter.

And they went to bed.

In the morning the sun was shining brightly in through the windows, and they got ready to go. They drew lots as to which of them should carry the barrel organ, and the lot fell on the tailor. But – what next? No sooner had the tailor swung the barrel organ on to his back than he vanished, and in his place stood a charming little carriage, with the barrel organ inside.

'All the better!' cried the hunter. And he got between the shafts to draw the carriage along. And – what next again? – no sooner had the hunter put himself between the shafts than he turned into a dappled horse, with bridle and collar and reins all complete.

So the smith seized the reins, jumped onto the carriage and drove off.

Now he was in luck. He had horse, carriage, and barrel organ. He travelled from village to town, from town to village. He played the barrel organ and went round with the hat. He collected many pennies: enough to keep him in food and clothing. And in every town and in every village he sat in a tavern, to eat and drink and tell his story.

And though the people liked to hear him tell his story, nobody would believe it.

And you and I – perhaps we don't believe it either?

7 · *Vasilissa Most Lovely*

A merchant and his wife had one little daughter, called Vasilissa, beautiful and good. But when Vasilissa was eight years old her mother fell ill, so ill that no doctor could cure her. And one morning the mother called Vasilissa to her bedside and said, 'My darling little daughter, I have something to give you.' And she took from under her pillow a small doll. 'This doll,' said she, 'was given to me at your christening by a fairy. Keep it carefully and show it to no one. But when trouble comes to you, as come I fear it will, give the doll something to eat, and ask her advice. She will tell you what you must do. And so goodbye, my little darling, and may heaven bless you!'

Then the mother kissed Vasilissa and died.

Now the merchant, Vasilissa's father, had often to travel about the country on his business. And he thought, 'I must take another wife, so that there may be someone to look after my little girl when I am away from home.'

And the merchant married again. His choice fell upon a handsome widow who had two daughters of her own, not very much older than Vasilissa.

'Now you will have playmates, my little one,' he said to Vasilissa, 'and a new mother to look after you. So now all will be well.'

But alas, all was not well. The stepmother was jealous of Vasilissa because she was so much more beautiful than her own two daughters, who were spoilt, bad-tempered things. And as the three girls grew, so the difference between them became more and more marked. Everyone loved Vasilissa, nobody liked her two stepsisters, and this so enraged the stepmother that she bullied Vasilissa, turning her out of her pretty bedroom to sleep in a garret under the roof, making her do all sorts of hard work, and dressing her in shabby old clothes; whilst her own two daughters flaunted themselves in silks and satins, and ordered Vasilissa about, and jeered at her.

Indeed, life would have become quite unbearable for Vasilissa if it had not been for her doll. But in the evening, when all were abed, Vasilissa would lock herself into the garret, take the doll out of her pocket, feed it with some dainty scraps of food that the stepsisters had left on their plates, and say, 'There, little doll, eat and listen to my grief. I live in my father's house, but I have no happiness. My stepmother beats me, my stepsisters bully me – teach me how to live! Even now I may not sleep, for I have much work still to do; and in the morning I must rise before the sun and light the stove, and sweep the kitchen, and weed the garden.'

And then the doll would answer, 'Go to bed, Vasilissa, sleep without a care. The morning is wiser than the evening. In the morning you shall run out into the sunshine and pick flowers, for all the work shall be done for you.'

And as the doll said, so it was. And despite all the stepmother's bullyings, and the stepsisters slaps and pinches, Vasilissa grew every year stronger and healthier and more beautiful; whilst her stepsisters grew uglier and dumpier, and pasty with idleness and over-eating.

So the years passed. The three girls were now growing up, and the stepmother was on the look-out for suitors for her two daughters. But not a lad would look at them: all the young men in the town came courting the lovely Vasilissa. And the stepmother foamed with rage. 'Go away!' she would scream; 'we do not marry the youngest before her elder sisters!'

'I must get rid of that girl, I must get rid of that girl, I must and *will* get rid of that girl!' the stepmother muttered.

So, with her two daughters, the stepmother formed a plan. One evening, when the merchant, Vasilissa's father, was away on a long journey, the stepmother set all three girls to work: one of her daughters to make lace, the other to knit stockings, and Vasilissa to spin. (And didn't Vasilissa marvel to see her two stepsisters so willing to work!)

'You must finish your tasks before you go to bed,' said the step-mother.

Then she threw water on the fire, and blew out all the candles but one. 'Waste comes to want,' said she, 'and one candle is light enough.'

'Oh yes, dear mother, quite enough,' said one stepsister.

And 'Quite light enough,' said the other stepsister.

And again Vasilissa wondered.

So then the stepmother went off to bed; and the three girls sat working. But the candle was burning down, and by and by it guttered and went out. Now there was no light at all in the room.

'What are we to do?' said the elder stepsister. 'We can't finish our work in the dark!'

'And we *must* finish it,' said the second stepsister. 'So someone must go and get a light from a neighbour.'

'But all the neighbours will be in bed by this time!' said the elder stepsister.

'The old witch Baba Yaga won't be in bed,' said the second step-sister. 'She sits up all night.'

'Well then, Vasilissa, you are the youngest, and you can run the fastest; so be off with you to the Baba Yaga and borrow a candle,' said the elder stepsister.

And they pushed Vasilissa out of the room and out through the front door, locking the door behind her.

So there stood Vasilissa in the darkness outside the house, not knowing what to do. For the Baba Yaga, who lived in a hut in the nearby forest, was a terrible old witch, who, it was said, ate up all who came her way, as if they were so many chickens.

'I cannot go, I dare not go,' thought poor Vasilissa. And she took her doll out of her pocket. 'Here is a biscuit I have saved for your supper, little doll,' she said. 'Eat and listen to my grief! They are sending me to the Baba Yaga. The Baba Yaga will eat me. What can I do?'

The doll ate up the biscuit, and then said, 'Don't be frightened, little Vasilissa. Having me with you, you may safely go anywhere. See, I will light your path.'

Then the doll's eyes lit up like two bright lamps. And Vasilissa, taking courage, went on her way into the dark forest.

She went, went, went; for hours she went. And suddenly she heard the sound of horse's hoofs, and a man came galloping towards her. The man's face was white, his clothes were white, the horse was white, the harness was white.

'The day breaks,' cried the man as he galloped past Vasilissa. 'And soon the sun will rise!'

Vasilissa walked on. Now it was not quite dark in the forest: she could just make out the shape of the trees; and by and by she again heard the sound of galloping hoofs, and another horseman came riding towards her. This horseman's hair seemed all one flame of red, he was dressed in red, and he rode on a red horse

'The sun, the sun, the sun is rising!' cried this second horseman as he galloped past.

And now through the forest shone rays of light, flickering on the leaves, and brightening the tree branches and the mossy trunks.

Vasilissa walked on. All through the day she walked, and came in the evening to a clearing. There in the clearing was the Baba Yaga's hut. All round the hut stood a high fence made of human bones; and on every upright post of the fence was a skull.

The lovely Vasilissa stood and shivered with fright. Then she again heard the sound of galloping hoofs, and along came riding a horseman dressed in black, wearing a black mask, and seated on a coal-black horse. The horseman galloped up to the high fence, the horse gave a leap, and suddenly it became so dark that Vasilissa could see nothing.

And then, as suddenly, all the eye sockets of the skulls on the fence began to blaze, and the whole clearing shone as brightly as if it had been noonday.

Now in the forest there arose a terrible noise. The branches of the trees clashed together, the leaves fell down, dry as wrinkled paper.

And through the forest came driving the Baba Yaga. In a mortar she rode, with a pestle she urged on the mortar, with a hearth-broom she swept up its traces from the ground. She rode up to the gate in the fence, she stopped. Her long nose sniffed here, sniffed there. 'Blood! Blood!' she shrieked. 'I smell Russian blood! Who is here? Who? Who?'

Then Vasilissa walked up to that old witch, the Baba Yaga, and curtsied low. 'It is I, Vasilissa, little grandmother,' she said. 'At home we sit in darkness, and my stepsisters have sent me to you to beg a light, if of your kindness you can spare one.'

'Oh yes!' said the Baba Yaga. 'I know your stepsisters – and one day they'll know me! Aah, ha, ha, ha! Now *you* are here, you must stay and you must work. If you work well, maybe I will give you a light. . . . Or maybe I will eat you. Who can tell?'

Then the Baba Yaga, that old witch, turned to the fence and screamed out, 'Hey, my strong bolts, unlock! Open, my wide gates, open yourselves!'

At once the gates flew open, and the Baba Yaga drove through, shrieking at Vasilissa to follow her. And after Vasilissa had passed through the gates, they shut again with a deathly crash.

The Baba Yaga scrambled out of the mortar and gave it a kick. 'Be off with you!' she screamed. Then the mortar disappeared, and the Baba Yaga went into the hut, dragging Vasilissa after her.

'Now,' said she, 'I want to eat. Serve up what's in the oven, fetch wine from the cellar, lay the table.' And all this Vasilissa did. There was enough meat in the oven to feed six people; but the Baba Yaga gobbled it all up, and drank down six flagons full of wine. But she gave Vasilissa only a crust of bread and a cheese rind.

So, after she had finished eating, the Baba Yaga yawned, opening her great mouth so wide that Vasilissa could see all down her red throat. 'Now,' said she, 'I am going to bed. You can sleep in the cellar, or anywhere else you fancy. But don't you think to run away! My skulls are good watch-dogs, and their jaws are strong. Ah ha! What they chase they tear to pieces! Tomorrow I shall be away all day. Whilst I am away, you must clean up the yard, sweep out the hut, wash this pile of dirty linen, starch, dry, and iron it. Also in the corn bin you will find two sorts of grain mixed up, wheat and oats. These you must separate into two heaps. You must also cook me a nice supper – the food's in the larder. And if all is done by the time I return, I won't eat you. But if all is *not* done, I'll tear the flesh off you, and stick your bones into my fence!'

Then the Baba Yaga screeched with laughter, and went to her bed. Very soon her snores shook the hut.

Vasilissa took the doll from her pocket, gave it some meat that the Baba Yaga had left on her plate, and whispered, 'Ah, little doll, what can I do?'

And the doll answered, 'Do not fear, lovely Vasilissa. Say your prayers and lie down to sleep. The morning is wiser than the evening. And I, your doll, can help you out of worse troubles than these.'

So then Vasilissa dried her eyes, and lay down before the kitchen fire and slept. And when she woke in the morning, the Baba Yaga was stamping out into the yard. Vasilissa looked through the window and saw that the eyes of the skulls were fading out. And then, with a flash and a glitter, the white horseman came galloping past, and the sky lightened. The Baba Yaga gave a shrill whistle, and there in the yard appeared the mortar, the pestle and the hearth brush. Next moment the red horseman went flashing by outside the fence, and the sun rose. The Baba Yaga sat herself in the mortar and rode out of the yard and into the forest. With the pestle she urged on the mortar, with the hearth-brush she swept away its traces from the ground. Then the branches of the trees crashed together, the leaves fell from them dry as wrinkled paper, the Baba Yaga rode away through the forest: and again everything was silent.

Now which of the tasks should Vasilissa begin on? She looked about her – and behold, every task was done! The dishes were washed and put up on a shelf, the floor was swept, the yard was cleaned, the linen, washed, starched and ironed, lay neatly folded on a chair; the wheat and the oats were separated into two heaps, and not a grain of the one was mixed with a grain of the other.

Vasilissa took the doll from her pocket, and gave it some breakfast. 'Ah, my dear, my darling doll,' said she, 'you are my deliverer! You have saved me!'

'Now you have nothing to do but prepare the Baba Yaga's supper,' said the doll, climbing back into Vasilissa's pocket. 'So keep up your heart, my little one! If it is not a pleasant place to be in, still we must make the best of it, you and I!'

So Vasilissa spent a restful day, and towards evening she set about cooking the Baba Yaga's supper. Now it began to grow dark. Outside, beyond the fence, the black rider on the black horse went galloping by. And all along the fence the eyes of the skulls were shining.

Then the trees in the forest crashed their boughs, the leaves fell crackling down, and through the forest came the Baba Yaga, and rode into the yard. With the pestle she urged on the mortar, with the hearth-brush she swept up its traces from the ground. 'Well, and is the work done, is it done?' she screamed at Vasilissa, who stood at the door looking out.

'Yes, the work is done,' said Vasilissa. 'Be pleased to look for yourself, little grandmother.'

The Baba Yaga inspected everything, hoping to find something to scold about. 'Well, very good!' she said at last. Then she gave a shriek, 'You, my faithful servants, my bosom friends, grind my wheat!'

And immediately there appeared three pairs of hands. The hands seized on the wheat, and carried it outside; and the Baba Yaga sat down to supper.

'You have done well today,' she said to Vasilissa. 'See that tomorrow you do well also. You will sweep and clean; and also you will take the poppy seed out of the bin over there. Someone has thrown earth into that bin, and now earth and poppy seeds are all mixed up. You must clean the seeds free of earth to the least little grain. If there is one little speck of earth left among the seed I shall eat you for my tomorrow's supper.'

So spoke the Baba Yaga, and having gobbled up the food Vasilissa had prepared for her, she went to her bed and next moment was snoring. Then Vasilissa took the doll from her pocket and fed it. And when the doll had eaten, it said, 'Say your prayers, Vasilissa, and lie down to sleep: the morning is wiser than the evening.'

So Vasilissa slept peacefully, sure now that the doll would help her out of all her troubles.

In the morning the Baba Yaga set off again in her mortar; and again Vasilissa had only to look round her, and behold all her tasks were already done. And in the evening, when the Baba Yaga came back, she could find fault with nothing. She went over to the bin where the poppy seed lay cleaned of earth; she clapped her hands and screamed, 'Now, my faithful servants, my bosom friends, press the oil from the seeds!'

Immediately there appeared the three pairs of hands. And the hands took up the poppy seeds and carried them away out of sight.

Then Baba Yaga sat down to her supper, and Vasilissa stood silent.

'Why do you stand there like a dumb girl?' said the Baba Yaga. 'Have you nothing to say to me?'

'I did not dare to speak,' said Vasilissa. 'But if you please there is something I should like to ask you.'

'Well, ask then!' shrieked the Baba Yaga, 'But it is not every kind of question that comes to good. The more you know, the older you grow. And the older you grow the uglier you become. Have you considered that, Vasilissa?'

'I should like to ask, if you please,' said Vasilissa, 'who the white horseman is – the white horseman who galloped past me in the forest.'

'That is Dawn, my bright Dawn,' said the Baba Yaga.

'And the red horseman?' said Vasilissa timidly. 'Who is he?'

'That is the Sun, my red rising Sun,' said the Baba Yaga.

'And the black horseman?' said Vasilissa.

'Ah ha! That is Night, my dark Night,' said the Baba Yaga. 'They are all my faithful servants. And what is your next question?'

Vasilissa thought of the three pairs of hands. But she was silent.

'Well,' shouted the Baba Yaga, 'why are you not asking anything more?'

'Because, little grandmother, you said yourself that to know too much is soon to grow old.'

'Ha!' said the Baba Yaga. 'You would not grow old here. Because if people ask too many questions I eat them. But now I will ask *you* something. How have you managed to do all the work I set you?'

'The blessing of my mother helped me,' said Vasilissa.

'What!' screamed the Baba Yaga. 'So that's it, is it? Get out of my sight, you blessed daughter. I can't do with blessed ones!' And she grabbed her broom and pushed Vasilissa out of the hut, and across the yard, and outside the hideous fence.

Then she seized one of the lighted skulls from the fence, crammed it on to a stick, and thrust it into Vasilissa's hand, screaming, 'Here is the light for your stepmother's daughters. Take it, take it! After

all it's what they sent you for, and though they hoped I should eat you, I have not eaten you, and I shall not eat you! I eat nothing blessed! Go from my sight, go – go! Your mother's blessing stings my bones!'

So with the skull to light her way, and with the doll safe in her pocket, Vasilissa set off through the forest for home. First it was black night in the forest, then came the white horseman riding by: it was dawn, and the light in the skull went out. Then came the red horseman riding by: the sun rose, and light glittered among the trees. And still Vasilissa was going, and by and by it was twilight, and then it was night again: the black horseman came riding through the forest, and the eyes of the skull lit up. And still Vasilissa was going, and it was very lonely and very silent. And though she took the doll out of her pocket once or twice, she had no food to give it, and so it never said a word.

On she went and on, and in the evening of the second day, came at last to her home.

But what was this? The house was in darkness. The stepmother and her daughters had had no light all the time that Vasilissa had been away: every light they lit immediately went out; and though they had tried to borrow lights from the neighbours, those lights, too, went out, as soon as they were brought into the house. So now the stepmother snatched the skull from Vasilissa, carried it into the parlour, and set it on the table.

'You've been long enough bringing it,' she said to Vasilissa.

'And what a hideous thing it is now you have brought it!' said the eldest stepsister.

'Couldn't you find anything better than that?' said the second stepsister. 'I'd be ashamed. . . .'

But the skull glared at them with its burning eyes and jumped off the table. They were so frightened that they ran out of the room. The skull bounded after them. They ran into the kitchen. The skull bounded after them. They ran from room to room. The skull bounded after them. They ran upstairs, downstairs. The skull bounded after them. They ran out of the house. The skull bounded after them. They ran into the forest. The skull bounded after them.

And its eyes burned brighter and brighter, until they were gone into the depths of the forest.

It is said that the skull chased them till they came to the Baba Yaga's hut, and that the Baba Yaga immediately swallowed them all three. But whether their end came that way, or some other way – who knows? All we do know is that the stepmother and her two daughters were never seen again, and that when the merchant, Vasilissa's father, came home from his travels, he found her alone with her doll.

It is said that when the merchant next went travelling, he took Vasilissa with him. It is also said that when Vasilissa was quite grown up the young Tsar fell in love with her and married her. So Vasilissa, most lovely, became Empress of Russia. And all ended well.

8 · The Pick Handle

Three girls, the daughters of Makame the witch-doctor, went out into the fields to play. And there were cannibals in that country.

So one of the girls said, 'My sisters, what shall we do if the cannibals come? If the cannibals come, I will use the enchantment given me by Makame, and change myself into a mouse, and creep away under the grass.'

The second girl said, 'Yes, I will use the enchantment given me by Makame, and change myself into a bee, and fly off among the flowers.'

The third girl said, 'And I will use the enchantment given me by Makame, and change myself into a pick handle.'

'Then you'll not be able to run away,' said the first girl.

'But you'll be safe enough,' said the second girl; 'because nobody wants to kill and eat a pick handle!'

And they laughed, and went on playing.

Then came the cannibals, beating their drums and shouting. What did they see? They saw a mouse creeping away under the grass, they saw a bee flying away among the flowers, and they saw a pick handle lying on the ground.

Said one cannibal, 'This pick handle shall be mine!'

Said another cannibal, 'No use a handle without a pick.'

Said the first cannibal, 'I shall take it away.'

The other cannibals said, 'All right. You take it.'

So the cannibal carried the pick handle home with him, and tossed it into his outhouse.

After that, all the cannibals went to bed. They slept.

Next day the men were sitting in the men's court, and their wives were working. The wives heard the pick handle speaking in the outhouse:

> *'Little mouse, little bee, little mouse, little bee,*
> *They were afraid, afraid and left me.*
> *They said little pick handle would not be killed,*
> *Little mouse, little bee, little mouse, little bee!'*

The wives went to the men's court and said, 'Man, the pick handle in your outhouse is speaking.'

The cannibal said, 'A pick handle cannot speak.'

The wives said, 'Come, and you will hear.'

So the cannibal went to listen. And the pick handle spoke again:

> *'Little mouse, little bee, little mouse, little bee,*
> *They were afraid, afraid and left me.*
> *Little mouse, little bee, little mouse, little bee,*
> *They said little pick handle would not be killed,*

The cannibal said, 'Oh, oh, the pick handle *is* speaking!'

And he went back into the men's court, crying out, 'Men, men, my pick handle is speaking!'

The cannibals said, 'Ho! Ho!'

The cannibal said, 'But truly it *is* speaking. Come, and you will hear.'

So they all got up, and went to the door of the outhouse. They listened. They heard:

> *'Little mouse, little bee, little mouse, little bee,*
> *They were afraid, afraid, and left me.*
> *Little mouse, little bee, little mouse, little bee,*
> *They said little pick handle would not be killed,*
> *Little mouse, little bee, little mouse, little bee!'*

The cannibals said, 'Indeed, indeed, that pick handle is speaking!'

They went away. Not one of them would go into the outhouse.

By and by the sun set. The cannibals ate their supper. They went to bed. They slept.

In the early morning the voice in the outhouse began again:

> *'Little mouse, little bee, little mouse, little bee,*
> *They were afraid, afraid, and left me.*
> *Little mouse, little bee, little mouse, little bee,*
> *They said little pick handle would not be killed.*
> *Little mouse, little bee, little mouse, little bee!'*

And now, as it spoke, the pick handle was rolling itself this way and that way. It rolled itself against the outhouse door. It rose up and gave the door a bang – the door flew open. It rolled itself out through the open door. It went on rolling. . . .

And when the people went out in the morning, they found that the pick handle had departed. Yes, it had gone. But they did not know where it had gone.

9 · The Princess in the Mountain

There was a young musician – Ambrose was his name – and one day he put all the money he possessed into a little purse, tucked his fiddle under his arm, and walked off into the world to seek his fortune. And as he was walking along, he saw a lad sitting by the side of the road. The lad was holding a log of wood against his left shoulder, and a stick in his right hand; and he was drawing the stick to and fro across the log, and humming a tune.

'Pretending to make music?' says Ambrose.

'Pretending it is,' says the lad. 'But if I had a real fiddle, and knew how to play it, I'd have all the world listening.'

'Would you indeed?' says Ambrose. 'Then throw away that log and come with me. I'll teach you to play.'

The lad, whose name was Janko, threw down the log and jumped up. He and Ambrose walked along together. They came to a town, Ambrose took a room in a tavern, and that same evening he put his fiddle into Janko's hand and began teaching him to play. Janko learned quickly. It wasn't long before he could play even better than Ambrose himself. Then Ambrose emptied all the money out of his purse, and bought Janko a fiddle of his own.

'Now, my lad,' says he, 'I've spent my last penny; so we must both of us make music to earn our bread.'

And that's what they did. They wandered on through towns and villages, playing their fiddles and passing round the hat. But they didn't earn much, and often they went hungry.

Now one day, as they were going from one town to the next, their way led through a forest, and there came a great storm of wind. The branches were tossing and groaning, the leaves were falling from the trees and whirling along the ground; and something that wasn't a leaf came spinning against Ambrose's foot. He picked up that something. What was it? A tiny, tiny green cap.

'My cap, my cap, give me my cap!' shrilled a tiny, tiny voice. And there at Ambrose's foot stood a tiny, tiny man, scarce six inches high, holding up his tiny hands.

'Here you are, little friend,' said Ambrose. And he stooped to put the tiny green cap into the tiny man's tiny hands.

The tiny man put the tiny cap on his tiny head, and held it there with both hands. He stamped his tiny foot. 'Be off with you, wind, you great bully!' he shrilled. And immediately the wind rushed away out of the forest, and everything was still.

The tiny man was smiling now. 'Thank you, friend Ambrose,' said he. 'That north-west wind is my enemy. He knows that my power lies in my cap, and so he is always trying to steal it from me. . . . But

what can I do? he screamed, getting all worked up again. 'I can't go through life holding my cap on with both my hands!'

'If that's all your trouble, it's soon remedied,' said Ambrose. And he took a lace out of one of his shoes, passed the lace over the tiny man's cap, and knotted it firmly under the tiny man's chin.

'There you are,' said he. 'The wind won't undo *that* knot in a hurry!'

The tiny man was delighted. He clapped his tiny hands and turned several somersaults. Then he felt for his cap. 'It's still on my head!' he shrilled. 'Still on my head, still on my head! . . . For that kind deed I'll make both your fortunes, that I will! Say "*Pr-rit!*" friend Ambrose. Say it, say it!'

'*Pr-rit!*' said Ambrose, laughing.

What happened? Ambrose disappeared; and there stood a great brown bear.

'Say "Pr-rat!"'' shrilled the tiny man.

'Pr-rat!' growled the bear.

What happened? The bear disappeared; and there stood Ambrose. The tiny man began hopping from one foot to the other, and singing in a voice as shrill as a grasshopper's:

> 'Pr-rit! Pr-rat!
> *Remember that!*
> *Man to bear, bear to Man,*
> *Use your wits if you can.*
> *My debt's paid,*
> *Your fortune's made!*'

Then the tiny man clapped his tiny hands, turned several more somersaults, and vanished.

'As-tonishing!' said Ambrose.

'Amazing!' said Janko.

'Though I don't see how it's going to make our fortunes,' said Ambrose.

'Nor I,' said Janko. 'But we could earn a few coins with a dancing bear show.'

'So we could,' said Ambrose.

And they walked on through the forest, where all was now still, with scarce a leaf stirring.

Beyond the forest they came to a town. So Ambrose said '*Pr-rit!*' turned into a bear, and followed at Janko's heels through the streets to the town square. Then Janko played his fiddle, and Ambrose-bear danced. He did tricks, too. He did whatever Janko told him to do. 'Oh see!' cried the people, 'the bear understands everything that's said to him! You'd almost think he was a human being!' And when the bear stood on his hind legs and went round with Janko's hat – well, it wasn't long before the hat was full of coins.

Janko and Ambrose-bear wandered on from town to town, and everywhere the crowds gathered round them, laughing and cheering, and tossing coins into Janko's hat. Now they never went hungry – they could have all the food they needed! They bought some fine clothes for themselves, too. Ambrose-bear carried the clothes in a box as they journeyed; and Janko hid the box in one place or another when they drew near a town.

By and by in their journeyings they came to the king's city. The king heard about the marvellous bear, and he summoned Janko and the bear to come and perform before him. Janko fiddled; Ambrose-bear danced and did all his tricks. The king laughed and laughed.

Now you must know that the king had a beautiful young daughter; and he loved her so much that he wouldn't let her get married. He wanted to keep her always with him; so he built a little palace for her inside a mountain; and except for himself and one faithful old servant, no one knew where the entrance to the palace was.

That was bad enough of the king, to shut up the poor little princess. But he did something even worse. He made it known that any man who could find the princess should have her to wife. But if any man should come seeking for her and not find her, that man should lose his head. In this manner the king thought to frighten away all the princess's suitors; and in the end he did frighten them away; but not before a few gallant young princes had sought and not found her, and had had their heads chopped off by the selfish old king.

Of course the princess didn't like being shut up all by herself inside a mountain, and when the king went to visit her, as he did very often, she would weep and beg to be let out. The king wouldn't let her out, but he didn't want her to be unhappy, and he was always trying to think of ways to amuse her. Now he thought, 'She shall see the bear do his tricks, and surely that will make her laugh!'

So he said to Janko, 'Is the bear gentle?'

'Gentle as a lamb,' says Janko.

'He won't bite or anything?' says the king.

'Not he!' says Janko.

'Well, I'll keep him here for a while,' says the king. 'And you can go and amuse yourself in the town.'

Then he gave Janko a gold coin, and told him to come back in three hours. Janko went away. The king called his faithful old servant, and the two of them set off for the mountain, the faithful servant leading Ambrose-bear on a rope.

Half way up the mountain there was a little door, so cunningly disguised that it looked like a grey rock. At the foot of the door was a flat stone, and under the stone was a key. The faithful servant took the key from under the stone and unlocked the door. Now they were in a passage, and at the end of the passage was another door. Beside this door stood the stuffed figure of an old man with a long beard. The servant gave a pull at the beard, and the key of the door fell out of it. He unlocked the door, and they all went through into yet another passage. At the end of this passage was a third door, guarded by a lion. The servant tweaked the lion's mane, and the lion spat a key out of his mouth. The servant took the key and unlocked this third door, and they all went through. Now they were in a pretty room, where the princess sat in a golden chair, singing to herself and playing on a zither.

And no sooner did Ambrose-bear hear the music than he reared up on his hind legs and began to dance.

'Oh, oh!' cried the princess. 'Oh, what fun!' She clapped her hands and the zither slid to the floor. What did Ambrose-bear do then? He picked up the zither and played a little tune on it: *tee tok, tee tumpty, tee tok ty*. Then he bowed, handed the zither back to the princess, and stood on his head. He did all sorts of tricks, turned somersaults and catherine wheels, walked on his two front feet with his hind legs in the air, picked up a candlestick and balanced it on his nose, bowed to the princess, danced again: and all the time he was saying to himself, 'Oh, how beautiful she is! How beautiful!' And by and by, there she was, holding him by one paw, and dancing with him.

'Oh, please, Papa, please, please, Papa, don't take him away!' cried the princess. 'Let me keep him for a little while!'

The king was delighted to see her happy; and he agreed to let the bear stay. Then he went away, taking the servant with him, saying that the servant should come back and fetch the bear in two hours time.

No sooner had the king and the servant gone away, than Ambrose-bear began to speak: 'Oh, lovely king's daughter, I am no bear, but a human being like yourself. In a moment you shall see me as I truly am. Don't be frightened, little princess! Say you will trust me, for I think I see a way to release you from this prison.'

The princess was just a little frightened, but she was also excited and pleased, for she had seen no one but the king and the old servant for a long, long time. So she said, 'Yes, I will trust you.' And Ambrose-bear said 'Pr-rat!' There he was now, as handsome a lad as you could wish to see, and smiling at her.

'O-oh!' said the princess. 'O-oh!' And that's all she could say for a little while. But by and by she was chatting to him as if she had known him all her life. And as to Ambrose, he was now as deep in love as any lad could be.

'And you will free me?' said the princess.

'Yes, I will free you,' said Ambrose.

But then they heard footsteps outside the door: and Ambrose had scarcely time to say 'Pr-rit!' and turn into a bear, before the door opened, and there was the old servant once again.

So the princess whispered, 'Come back soon,' into the furry ear of Ambrose-bear, and the faithful servant led him away to the king's palace, and handed him over to Janko.

That night Ambrose and Janko slept in a forest, where Janko had hidden their box of new clothes. And next morning Ambrose dressed himself up finely, and went once more into the city. First he went to a bath-house, and then he went to a barber's; and so – washed, shaved, curled and scented, and looking like any young lord in his fine new clothes – off with him to the king's palace, where he announced himself as Lord Ambrose of Outland, a suitor for the princess.

The king looked Ambrose up and down; he curled his lips, raised his eyebrows, shrugged his shoulders, and said, 'Well, my fine fellow, if you care to lose your head, it's all one to me.'

But Ambrose said, 'I will bring you the princess before sundown.' And he bowed, and made to go.

'Stop a minute!' said the king. 'You won't find the princess, and then you'll run away to escape your punishment! No, no, I'm not letting you out of my sight! Where you go this day, I go with you.'

'As you wish,' said Ambrose.

Well, they set off together. And, my word, didn't Ambrose lead the king a dance – rummaging through the palace, and up and down the city streets, into every cellar, and out into the field, and poking into barns and stables and pigsties, pulling haystacks to pieces and flinging hay in the king's face, and leading him into swamps where he got stuck in the mud, and hauling him out of the mud with no gentle hand, for he thought the king deserved all the punishment he could give him.

So at last, quite worn out, the king said, 'You know you're beaten. Now we'll go back to the palace, and I will hand you over to the executioner.'

But Ambrose said, 'All in good time, your majesty. I see a little mountain yonder which we have not yet explored.'

And he went to the mountain and began to climb, and the king went stumbling after him.

'What is the sense of this?' panted the king. 'There is nothing here but bare rocks. How could a princess live among bare rocks?'

'People have lived in stranger places,' said Ambrose. 'Sometimes if you knock on bare rocks, bare rocks will open. . . . And here is a rock that looks very like a door.'

'Well then, knock on it, you fool!' shouted the king, who was getting anxious.

Ambrose knocked on the rock. Of course the rock didn't open. Ambrose kicked the rock, he was teasing the king. He made to stumble, he fell on his hands and knees, he snatched at the flat stone that lay under the rock, and pushed the stone aside.

'Ah ha! What's this? It looks like a little key! It *is* a little key! If there's a little key, there should be a little keyhole. Can you find a little keyhole, my gracious king? No? But perhaps I can! Under this bunch of lichen, for instance? Just let's have a look. Well, did you ever – here *is* a little keyhole! Now if the key should fit the keyhole, wouldn't that surprise you, my gracious king? And see – the key does fit, and the door swings open. So in we go!'

'I'm not going in!' shouted the king. 'It may be a robbers' den!'

'But *I* am going in,' said Ambrose, stepping through the door.

And of course the king had to follow.

'I'll have your head for this! I'll have your head!' muttered the king.

But Ambrose went on, and came to the second door, and to the stuffed figure of the old man with the long beard.

'Good day to you, Sir Long Beard!' says Ambrose. 'May I trouble your worship to hand over the key of this door? What, you won't? Very well – take that!' He gave the figure a blow that sent it toppling; and the key fell out of its beard.

'If you don't stop this tomfoolery, I'll have you hanged, drawn, and quartered!' shrieked the king. But Ambrose laughed. He unlocked this second door and stepped through; and the king followed, shaking with rage.

Now they came to the third door, guarded by the lion.

'Eat him up, my lion!' shouted the king. 'Eat up this insolent fellow!'

But the lion snarled at the king, whom he hated for keeping him shut up. Even before Ambrose had reached out to tweak his mane, he spat the key out of his mouth and made off, out through the second door, out through the first door, away down the mountain and away and away to freedom in the forest.

Ambrose laughed. He unlocked this third door, and came into the pretty room where the princess sat in her golden chair, playing on her zither and singing softly to herself. And didn't the princess jump up and clap her hands!

'Good afternoon, Papa!' says she. 'And good afternoon to you, stranger! Have you come to set me free?'

'Yes, I have come to set you free, and to claim my bride,' said Ambrose.

Then he took the princess by the hand and led her out of her prison and down the mountain to the palace. And the king staggered after them, grinding his teeth with rage.

The princess was all eager to have the wedding at once; and Ambrose wasn't less eager, you may be sure. But the king, the old rascal, wasn't going to lose his daughter without a struggle. So he summoned his favourite courtier, a sly mean fellow, called Ritter Rok, and asked him, 'How can I stop this wedding?'

'Easily enough,' said Ritter Rok. 'You know that your enemy, the King of the South, is raising an army against you, because you had his son's head cut off. Well now, there's a flail hanging on a beam in hell that would put any enemy army to flight; for whatever that flail touches it burns to a cinder. Send Ambrose to fetch that flail – he won't come back.'

'I'll do that!' said the king, greatly heartened. And he sent for Ambrose, and told him to go and fetch the flail.

'But we must get married first,' said the princess. 'For you promised, Papa!'

'Stupid girl!' snarled the king. 'How can we hold a wedding when there is an enemy on the march against us? No, no, the battle first, and the wedding afterwards.'

The princess went away. She shed bitter tears. And as she sat and wept – there was the tiny man in the green cap standing at her feet.

'Ho! ho! What's the matter here?' shrilled the tiny man.

'Oh,' sobbed the princess. 'My father is sending Ambrose to fetch the burning flail from hell. The flail will burn him to a cinder. He will die, and I shall die too, for I can't live without him!'

'No, he won't die,' said the tiny man. He clapped his tiny hands, and there in the princess's lap lay a big jar of green ointment.

'Let Ambrose rub himself all over with that ointment,' said the tiny man, 'and never a burn nor a scald will he get, even were he to step into the fiercest fire in hell.'

And then, even before the princess had time to thank him, the tiny man vanished.

The princess ran to Ambrose with the ointment, and he rubbed himself all over with it, and smeared it all over his clothes, too. After that, he kissed the princess goodbye and set off for hell. He travelled and travelled; he went a long, long way, but at last he came in sight of the walls of hell, and hurried to the gate, and knocked loudly.

'What do you want?' shrieked a hundred little devils, looking over the wall.

'I wish to speak to Satan,' says Ambrose, 'and I'll trouble you to open the gate.'

Well, they opened the gate, and let Ambrose in, and brought him to Satan, who sat on his burning throne, eating a mincemeat of poor lost souls. Satan looked hard at Ambrose, thinking to shrivel him up with the fire of his eyes. But Ambrose didn't flinch. So Satan, very astonished, asked him to his business.

'My business is soon told,' says Ambrose. 'I come for the loan of that flail I see hanging on the beam yonder, so that my king may give a thrashing to his enemies.'

'Well, well,' says Satan, 'your king is a good customer to me. He shall have the flail, and welcome. Just you hand it down,' says he to a young imp – giving that imp a wink of his eye, much as to say, 'Now we shall see some fun!'

So the imp climbed up to the beam and fetched down the flail, which was made of red-hot iron. The little rascal was grinning to think how it would burn the hands off Ambrose: but Ambrose had his hands well greased with the green ointment, and not a burn did he get.

'Thank you,' says he. 'And now, if you'll open the gate again, I'll be off and give you no more trouble.'

'Oh ho! says Satan. 'Is that the way of it, my fine fellow? But it's easier to get inside hell gate than to get out again. Now my lads, take that flail from him, and let him feel your claws in his skin!'

Then one devil ran up to make a grab at Ambrose; but Ambrose gave the devil a blow with the flail that knocked him backwards; and another devil ran up, and got a harder blow than the first one. And then a whole lot of devils set upon him; and it was *whack, whack* with the flail, and the devils falling about like ninepins, and howling fit to raise hell's roof. Even Satan himself couldn't hold Ambrose, because his clawed hands slipped off the ointment. And at last Satan shrieked, 'Open the gate – let the fool out! And woe betide any one of you who ever lets him in again!'

Then they ran to open the gate. Ambrose walked off in triumph, carrying the flail: and the devils, big and little, clambered up on to hell's walls and shrieked curses after him – which you may be sure he didn't trouble himself to notice.

When he got back to the king's palace, Ambrose laid the flail down on the stones in the courtyard, and warned everybody not to touch it for their lives. The king wasn't a bit pleased to see him. 'You'll have to think of some better way of getting rid of the tiresome fellow,' he said to Ritter Rok, 'or I'll have *your* head instead of his!'

'I'll make an end of him here and now!' bawled Ritter Rok. And he rushed to pick up the flail, thinking to strike Ambrose over the head with it. But his fingers had scarcely touched the flail when he let out a roar, and there he was dancing with pain, and flinging his arms about, and screaming. So Ambrose ran and caught Ritter Rok's hand in his own two, and rubbed them this way and that till the pain left them. And after that Ritter Rok went away and sulked, and didn't show his face again at court for a long time.

What happened next? Well, the princess came running out in her wedding dress. 'Papa,' says she, 'the priest is waiting in the royal chapel, and Ambrose has the ring. If you don't come *this instant*, Papa, I'll find someone else to give me away!'

So the king had to submit, and they held a fine wedding, with a fine feast to follow. The lad Janko brought his fiddle and played at the feast. He played sometimes so merrily, and again sometimes so sadly, that first the guests were all laughing, and then they were all wiping their eyes.

And the princess said, 'Dear Janko, you shall never leave us. You shall be my own music master. When I am joyful, your music shall tell of my joys; and if I am ever sorrowful, your music shall beautify my sorrows.'

Even the king's selfish heart was softened by Janko's playing. But what more than anything else put the king in a good temper was that when his enemy, the King of the South, heard about the flail, he was so frightened that he ordered his army to turn round and march home again.

As to the flail itself – well, what do you think? When Ambrose (having again well rubbed his hands with the green ointment) went out next morning to move it to some safer place, that flail had disappeared. And there, on the stones where it had lain, was a huge cleft, going down and down into a deep blackness. For the flail had burned itself a passage down through the earth, and gone back to its place in hell.

10 · Black, Red, and Gold

Once upon a time there lived a man and his wife who had a pretty home and enough money; they loved each other dearly, and yet they were not happy. Why was that? It was because they had no children.

Well, one stormy evening, they were sitting together before the fire and thinking of their sorrow, when there came a knock at the door.

The man went to open to door. 'Who is there?'

'A poor beggar, weary and hungry. Could you spare a bite to eat?'

'Oh yes, yes – come in!'

So the beggar came in. He was very lean, very old, very grey, and shaking with cold. The wife bustled about to get him food. The husband brought him a rug for his shoulders, drew up a chair for him close to the fire, took off his tattered old boots, and brought him a pair of slippers.

'I'm afraid I'm giving you a lot of trouble,' said the old man.

'Not at all, not at all,' said the husband. And 'Not at all, not at all,' said the wife. 'What is the world coming to, if we can't be neighbourly one to another? Come now, here's soup and meat and bread, and a glass of wine, so fall to and eat your fill.'

The old beggar ate and drank. Now he stopped shivering; he was warm and happy. 'But you, my dear good people,' he said. 'I see the marks of trouble on you – why is that?'

'Oh,' said the wife, and she burst into tears, 'it is because we have no children.'

'There is a remedy for most things,' said the beggar man. 'If you will allow me to sleep before your fire, perhaps in the morning I can give you good counsel.'

'You shall have a bed,' said the husband.

'No, no,' said the old man. 'The floor is the place for an old wanderer like me.'

So they wrapped him in blankets, and he lay down before the fire. Next moment he was asleep. And the husband and wife went to bed.

In the morning, when the wife came down into the kitchen, she found the old fellow bustling about. He had the fire going merrily, he had folded up his blankets, swept out the kitchen, and laid the table for breakfast.

'I have good news for you,' he said. 'It came to me in a dream, and my dreams never deceive me. Call your husband, that I may tell him what he must do.'

So the wife called her husband; and whilst she got the breakfast ready, her husband sat and listened to the old man's counsel.

'Now take heed, take heed,' said the old man. 'Have you any honey?'

'Yes,' said the husband, 'we have a jar full.'

'Then immediately after breakfast you must set out,' said the old man, 'taking the jar of honey with you, and also a candle and tinder-box. You must go through the forest that lies behind your house, and walk on until you come to a high mountain. This you must climb: half way up the mountain you will come to a cave. Set down the jar of honey at the entrance, light your candle, and go into the cave. It will be full of bees, but they will not harm you – they will smell the honey and fly out to it. In the cave you will find a woman who has hair of three colours: black, red, and gold. She will be fast asleep (she has already slept many thousands of years) but wake her, wake her! Tell her your trouble, and she will help you. Now will you trust me, and do as I say?'

'Yes, I will do as you say,' said the husband. But he thought, 'If it doesn't do any good, at least it can't do any harm.'

'I read your thought,' said the old man with a chuckle. 'But you must not doubt my dream.'

Then they all sat down to breakfast. And when they had eaten, the old fellow went on his way; and the husband took the jar of honey, a candle and a tinderbox, and set out, urged by his wife, who had more faith in the old fellow's dream than he had. The man walked through the forest, came to the mountain, and began to climb. Sure enough, half way up he found the entrance to a cave. He lit the candle and peered into the cave. Yes, there was a woman lying asleep. The woman had long hair of three colours: black, red, and gold, and there were bees crawling all over her. But when the man put down the jar of honey in the warm sun outside the cave, the bees buzzed up in a swarm and came flying out to settle on the honey jar: and the man went into the cave. He stepped over to the sleeping woman, and touched her gently. In a moment she was sitting up, brushing her three-coloured hair out of her eyes, and staring at him.

Long and long she looked at him without speaking. Then at last she said, 'I know why you have come. And since you have brought honey for my bees I will help you. Here is an apple for you, here also is a pear. If your wife eats the apple, she will have a son. If she eats the pear she will have a daughter. Now take three hairs from my head, one black, one red, and one gold. These I give as a christening present to your eldest child. Let them be twisted into a chain and hung about the child's neck – they will bring good fortune. Come, pull them out quickly and leave me, that I may sleep again.'

So the man pulled three hairs out of the woman's head, a black hair, and a red hair, and a gold hair, and having wrapped them, together with the apple and the pear, in his handkerchief, he thanked the woman and left her. And looking back, as he went out of the cave, he saw that she was already asleep again.

When he got home his wife came hurrying to the door, eager for news. And he showed her the apple and the pear. 'If you eat the apple you will give birth to a son; if you eat the pear you will give birth to a daughter – or so I was told.'

'O dear me!' said his wife. 'Haven't we tried this and that and the other thing, and nothing any good? Is it likely that an apple or a pear will help us? But it's a long time since I tasted a pear, and the sight of it makes my mouth water. So I may as well eat it.'

And eat the pear she did. But the apple she put on a shelf, and forgot about it.

Well now – would you believe it? After nine months the wife gave birth to the most lovely little golden-haired girl, and you can imagine what happiness that brought to both wife and husband. They called the baby Catalina, and the wife plaited the three hairs – the black, the red, and the gold – into a chain, and hung the chain round the baby's neck. And then one day the wife saw the apple on the shelf, and thought, 'Yes, I'll eat that too.' And she did eat it. And by and by she gave birth to a son, whom they called Johan.

'Now we have nothing more to wish for,' said the wife to the husband.

'No, nothing more,' said the husband to the wife; 'we are now blessed beyond measure!'

So the years passed happily, until Catalina's fourteenth birthday. And then a dreadful thing happened. Catalina had gone with little Johan down to the sea beach to look for shells and coloured stones, when she saw a big ship come sailing into the bay. The ship put out a boat, the men in the boat rowed ashore; and even whilst Catalina was wondering what manner of men they might be, the pirates (for such indeed they were) had snatched her up and carried her off to the ship. And little Johan, who had hidden behind a rock, and so was not seen by the pirates, ran home sobbing bitterly.

Now indeed there was no more happiness in the home of Catalina's parents. But we must leave them to their grief, and follow Catalina. The pirates carried her far over the sea to a town in a foreign land; and there they stood her up in the market-place, to sell her as a slave.

Poor Catalina, standing there to be stared at and bargained for by a crowd of cruel greedy men! But her luck did not entirely desert her. For among the slave buyers was a rich merchant whose own daughter had not long died. And when this rich merchant saw Catalina, she reminded him so much of his dear daughter that he out-bid all the rest of the buyers, paid a big price for her, and took her home.

'Little one,' he said, 'I think the good fairies must have sent you. You shall never be a slave. You shall be to me as my daughter.' And he dressed her in beautiful garments, and loved her, and treated her as his child. But though Catalina was grateful to him, she was not happy. She longed, oh how she longed, for her mother and her father, and for her brother Johan, and for her home! As for the

money the merchant gave her, she had no heart to spend it. She put it away in a drawer. But later on she was to find a use for it, as you will see.

Now amongst the slaves in the merchant's house, there were two young girls of Catalina's own age. One was a little black girl from Africa, with great brown eyes and black hair; the other was a slender Greek girl with beautiful red hair, who, since she was clever with her needle, the merchant set to embroidering his shirts. And these two girls were Catalina's particular friends.

So one day the little black girl came to Catalina and said, 'My heart is breaking. If I am not allowed to go home, I shall soon die. Dear Catalina, our master loves you as his daughter, and whatever you ask he will surely grant you. Do, do now go to him and beg that he will set me free!'

So Catalina went to the merchant and said, 'Master, the little black slave is quite ill with home-sickness. If she stays here I think she will soon die. Could you not set her free, and let her go home?'

But the merchant answered, 'Dear child, I am old and you are young. I know the ways of the world, and you do not. I give the little black girl a home, and I treat her kindly. If I let her wander off into the wicked world, she will most likely come to grief. Believe me, she is better where she is. But give her this ring as a token of how much I value her services.'

So Catalina took the ring and gave it to the little black girl. But the little black girl cast it down and wept. 'Ah, ah, what good is this bauble to me? If I cannot be free to go back to my parents and my brothers and sisters, I would rather die!' And she refused to eat or drink, and wept both day and night.

Catalina, too, shed tears of pity; but how to help the little black girl she could not think. And then one night she had a dream. In her dream there came to her a woman who had hair of three colours, black, red, and gold, and who wore a dress completely covered with bees. 'Catalina,' said the dream woman, 'untwist the black hair from the chain about your neck. Let the black hair fall to the ground, and you will be helped.'

So, when Catalina woke in the morning she remembered this

dream. And she took the chain from her neck, untwisted the black hair from the red and the gold, and threw the black hair on the ground.

Well now – what happened? The hair gave a hop and a wriggle: and there before Catalina stood a little dusky maiden, the very image of the little black slave girl.

'Mistress,' said the little dusky maiden, 'what shall I do?'

'Stay with us as a maid-servant,' said Catalina, 'and serve our master faithfully and well.'

'That I will do,' said the little dusky maiden.

Catalina fetched the ring which the real little black girl had thrown down, put it on the dusky maiden's finger, and said, 'When you see our master, thank him for this ring.'

'That I will do,' said the little dusky maiden.

Then with glad heart Catalina ran to her room, took a purse full of money from her drawer, hurried to where the real little black girl sat weeping, and said, 'Here is a purse full of money for you. Go quickly before our master wakes, make your way home, and may heaven bless you! I have found one to take your place.'

So the real little black girl set off joyfully for home. And the little dusky maiden, who had sprung from the black hair, worked in her place about the house. And the merchant never noticed any difference.

But now there was the young Greek slave girl, with the flaming red hair, and she too was weeping and lamenting. 'Oh, my mother, oh, my father,' wept the young Greek slave girl, 'oh, my dear brothers and sisters! How can I live without them? Oh, my little home on the hill among the olive trees! Shall I never see it again? Catalina, you are our master's darling. Go to him, go. Perhaps if you ask him he will set me free!'

So Catalina went to the merchant and said, 'Dear master, your Greek slave weeps day and night. Will you not set her free to go home to her people?'

But the merchant answered, 'Catalina, ever dear to me, and all the dearer for your kind heart, believe me, I know what is best. The Greek slave will console herself. Did you not ask me the other day to set the little black slave free? If I had done so, who knows what evil might have befallen her as she journeyed through the world? And see now, how she is working with a will, and merry as the day is long. Our young Greek slave will also soon console herself. Give her this gold necklace. And ask yourself if in all the world she could find a kinder or more considerate master.'

Catalina took the gold necklace to the little Greek slave, but the little Greek slave cast it from her and said, 'What good is a gold chain to me who must presently die of grief? Now I will do no more embroidery for my master! I will neither eat nor drink, nor work, nor play! I will lay me down and wait for death to set me free!'

And she lay down on her bed and turned her face to the wall.

That night Catalina dreamed again of the woman with the hair of three colours, black, red, and gold. 'Catalina,' said the dream woman, 'untwist the red hair from the chain about your neck. Let the red hair fall to the ground, and you will be helped.'

In the morning, Catalina did what the dream woman had told her. And no sooner had she cast the red hair on to the ground than there stood before her a slender red-haired maiden, the very image of the little Greek slave.

'Mistress,' said the red-haired maiden. 'What must I do?'

'Stay with us,' said Catalina, 'and embroider the master's shirts.'

'That I will do,' said the red-haired maiden.

Catalina fetched the gold chain which the merchant had given to the little Greek slave, hung it about the red-haired maiden's neck, and said, 'When you see our master, thank him for this chain.'

'That I will do,' said the red-haired maiden.

Then with glad heart Catalina fetched a purse full of money, ran to where the real little Greek maiden lay on her bed with her face to the wall. 'Get up, get up!' said Catalina, giving the Greek girl a shake. 'Here is a purse full of money for you. Go quickly, before our master wakes. Make your way home and may heaven bless you! I have found one to take your place.'

'And may heaven bless *you*!' cried the little Greek slave, springing up to embrace Catalina. And she took the purse and set off for home, without even stopping to comb out her red hair.

Now all went on as usual in the merchant's house. The little dusky maiden, who had sprung from the black hair, worked about the house, and laughed; the red-haired maiden, who had sprung from the red hair, sat at her embroidery frame and sang happily as she worked. The merchant saw no difference in either of the maidens, or in their work, except that it seemed to him they were working even better than ever. 'Little Greek,' said he to the one who sat at the embroidery frame, 'your embroidery gets more beautiful every day.'

'Ah, but you should just see how we embroider in my home land,' said the red-haired maiden. And she laughed.

'There you are,' said the merchant to Catalina, 'what did I tell you? My young slaves have consoled themselves. Now they are both as happy as the day is long.'

'Yes, as the day is long, dear master,' answered Catalina with a sigh.

For oh how long and weary did the days seem to her, and how gladly would she have run away, and wandered over all the world, if only she could at last have reached her home! 'But no,' she told herself. 'Has not my master said he loved me as his own child? If I left him, his heart would surely break!'

So the days went by, and the years went by, and Catalina was now quite grown up. Her master had given her a pretty room with a balcony that overlooked the harbour and the main street of the town. And one day she sat on the balcony watching the ships coming and going, and the busy scene on the quay, there came a young knight riding by on the road past the merchant's house.

'There goes one who may travel where he pleases,' thought Catalina. And she sighed.

It was only a little sigh, but somehow or other the young knight must have heard it, for he reined in his horse, glanced up, and seeing Catalina, so lovely, so sorrowful-looking, he swept off his hat, gave a bow and said, 'God greet you, Christian maiden!'

'God greet you, sir knight,' said Catalina.

'Ah,' said the knight, 'your voice is like music. What are you called?'

'I am called Far-From-Home, and I belong to a kind master,' said Catalina. 'And you, what are you called?'

'My name is Johan,' said the young knight. 'And I come from a land across the sea, where my father and mother are now awaiting my return. I am their only child, though once I had a sister, who was snatched away from me by pirates. I do not know whether she is alive or dead; but if she lives she must be about your age. And as I remember her, her hair was shining gold, just like yours.'

Then Catalina's heart gave a great leap, for she knew that this young knight must be her own brother – her little brother Johan, grown to be a man. But Johan's next words set her mind in a whirl, for he said, 'Shall I buy you free, Far-From-Home?'

Ah, if that were possible! 'But my master would not sell me for all the treasures in the world, because he loves me as his own daughter.'

'Well then, Far-From-Home, you must run away! You must come on board my boat, and I will take you to my mother.'

'Oh no, no, I cannot do that! If I went away my master's heart would break!'

'Better his heart should break than yours, beautiful Far-From-Home,' said Johan. 'Think! Think! You cannot willingly remain a slave! I must now go. But I offer you your freedom, and I will come again tomorrow for your answer.'

Then Johan rode on his way, and Catalina went back into the house, more unhappy, perhaps, than she had ever been in her life. What was she to do? If she told her brother who she really was, then surely he would take her away by force; and, if that happened, her good old master would surely die of grief. But to be free: to go home, to see her mother and father again, to live with them in happiness – ah, how she longed for that! She wept the whole night long, and could find no rest.

And next day, feeling that she must see her brother yet once again, she went to sit on the balcony, and waited and watched Yes, there he came, so handsome, so charming, her own dear Johan riding up the street.

'Far-From-Home, will you come away with me?'

And Catalina, who could scarcely speak for tears, answered, 'No, I cannot.'

'Now I shall come no more,' said Johan, 'for at dawn tomorrow we set sail. I will wave to you from the ship – the three-masted barque with the white lilies on her flag. Perhaps even yet you will come?'

But Catalina shook her head, and darted into the house.

'My dear master must not see me weeping,' she said to herself. And she tried hard to be merry. When her master noticed her red eyes and asked what ailed her, she told him she had caught a little cold. So he packed her off to bed, the dear good man, and sent her up one warm drink after another. But all that day, and all the following night, she lay thinking of her home that she would never see again, and of her mother and her father and of her brother Johan, whom she had found – only, it seemed, to lose again.

Very early next morning she rose and went up to the topmost storey of the house. Here a window opened on to a flat roof; and she climbed out through the window, and went to stand against a parapet from which she could see the harbour. Down there, amongst a crowd of craft big and little, was a three-masted barque with white lilies on her flag; and as the sun rose, this barque began to move slowly but surely out to sea. Yes, it was her brother's ship: she could see him quite clearly, standing on deck and looking towards the house. . . . Now he saw her, now he was waving, now Catalina was waving back. . . .

'Oh, brother, brother, goodbye, my brother!' And lo, even as she stretched out her arms, the chain round her neck, which now indeed consisted of only one golden hair, fell to the ground.

And no sooner had that golden hair touched the flagstones at her feet, than there stood before Catalina a maiden as like herself as if she had stepped out of a mirror.

'Mistress, what shall I do?'

'Oh, stay here, stay here with my master the merchant, love him and make him happy!' cried Catalina: and off with her, faster than she had ever run in her life, down the stairs, out of the house, and away to the harbour.

And from the ship which had already cleared the harbour, Johan saw her and said, 'Captain, turn back, I have forgotten something.'

'You should have said that sooner,' grumbled the captain. 'Now it is too late. We shall miss the favourable wind.'

'Yet turn back, turn back!'

'Well, so be it.'

So there was the ship back in harbour, and there was Catalina on the quay, and there was Johan leaping out to help her on deck.

'Didn't I tell you that you would think differently?' laughed Johan, as they put to sea again. . . .

That evening Johan and Catalina stood hand in hand leaning over the gunwale, watching the moonlight that flickered on the water.

'Far-From-Home,' said Johan, 'how would it be if you and I got married?'

'No, no!' said Catalina, 'I love you, I shall always love you, but I can never be your wife. I have not yet told you my real name. I am called Catalina.'

'That makes you all the dearer,' said Johan, 'for that was my sister's name.'

'Oh, Johan, dear Johan, I *am* your sister!'

And she told him all her story.

So happily, happily they sailed over the sea; and happily, happily Catalina came home to her mother and father. And that's the end of the story. Except, so we are told, Catalina by and by married a duke, and had three beautiful little daughters: one with black hair, one with gold hair, and one with hair the colour of the rising sun.

11 · The Knights of the Fish

You must know that there was once a countryman, and he was very poor. There came a day when his wife said to him, 'Husband, the larder is bare, and the cupboard is bare, and all we have between us and famine is one half loaf.'

So the countryman borrowed a fishing rod from a neighbour, and went to the stream to see if he could catch a fish for dinner. Almost at once he got a bite, and pulled in the most beautiful fish he had ever seen. The body of the fish was glistening white, its fins and tail shone with the seven colours of the rainbow, and it had large golden eyes. It was so beautiful that despite his hunger the man had a mind to throw it back into the water. He had taken it off the hook, and was stooping to drop it into the stream, when a little bubbly voice spoke from between his hands.

Yes, it was the fish speaking.

'Thank you for your kind thought, my friend. But I do not ask you to spare my life. You and your wife are very hungry, and I know it. Take me home and cook me; and when I am cooked cut me into eight pieces. Give two pieces to your wife, eat two yourself, bury two under the ashes of your hearth, and the remaining two lay in the earth, one at each corner of your hut. And may I bring you good fortune!'

The countryman did as the fish had bidden him. And though the fish was not very big, when he and his wife had eaten their share of it, their hunger had gone, and they felt as though they had had a splendid meal.

'It was certainly a magic fish,' said the countryman.

Magic indeed! Next morning, when the wife was sweeping the hearth, what should she find under the ashes, but two sacks full of gold pieces.

'Husband!' she cried. 'Husband, come and see what the fish has given us!'

How they rejoiced! They were poor no longer. The countryman was able to buy all the meadows that the stream flowed through; and he pulled down their hut and built a farmhouse in its place. He became a prosperous farmer, owning cattle and sheep and wheat fields and cabbage and turnip fields.

But that wasn't the end of their good fortune. By and by the wife gave birth to twin sons, exactly alike; and search the world through, you couldn't have found more beautiful or healthy babies.

At the same time as the twins were born, two slender trees sprang up, one at each side of the house, and the trees were of a kind that no man could give a name to.

The children grew, and the trees grew. And on the twins' sixth

birthday, the countryman saw some curious objects hanging among the branches of the little slender trees. He hurried to take down these objects – and what did he find they were? Two little helmets, two little breast-plates, two little lances, two little swords, and two little shields. The breast-plates were striped with the seven colours of the rainbow, and the shields bore a device of a white fish, arched by a rainbow.

'Wife!' he called. 'Wife, come and see what pretty things the fish has given to our children!'

He fastened the pieces of armour on to the two children, and the armour fitted them exactly. The children were delighted. They played at tournaments, and they became known near and far as the Little Knights of the Fish.

Then one day, when the countryman went into the meadows to drive in his cows, he saw two dappled foals grazing with the cattle. He left them there to graze; but as the days passed and nobody claimed them, he said to his wife, 'I think the foals must be another gift from the fish.' And he brought them in and groomed them, and gave them to the children. And the foals were so alike that no one knew which was which, except their two little masters.

The foals grew, the children grew, and the armour grew with them. The years went by, the children were now two strong, brave and handsome lads, the armour was now of a size to fit two fully grown men, and the foals were now two magnificent dappled horses. Moreover those horses didn't grow old; they remained in the pride of their strength to serve their masters.

And one day the first Knight of the Fish said to the second Knight of the Fish, 'Brother, I do not think we are meant to stay idling here. Surely, with these horses and this armour, we are meant to ride out into the world in quest of adventure.'

And the second Knight of the Fish answered, 'Yes, surely that is what we are meant to do.'

So the twins went to their father and said, 'Father, give us your blessing. We are going out into the world in quest of adventure.'

'Yes, my sons,' said the father, 'you must go where your destiny calls you.'

And he gave them his blessing, and so did their mother. And the Knights of the Fish set out.

They rode along the highway together, and a handsome pair they were, as alike as two peas in a pod, or two blades of grass, or two petals of a flower, or any things you can think of that are more alike than these things are.

By and by the highway forked into two roads, the one going east, the other west, and there the Knights of the Fish embraced and parted. For knights that ride in quest of adventure must ride alone.

The Knight who went east came by and by to a great city. The streets were filled with crowds of people dressed in black; and the people were all weeping, and tearing their hair, and putting ashes on their heads. When the Knight asked what was the matter, they only wept the more and cried, 'The princess! The princess!' Nor could he get one word of sense out of them. So at last he leaped from his horse, caught an old man by the sleeve, and said, 'I will not let you go until you tell me why you are all weeping.'

Then the old man told him that every year a beautiful girl was chosen by lot to be offered up to a fiery dragon; because the dragon's mother, who was the terrible old witch Albatroz, had put a curse on the city, and if they did not do as she bade them, every man, woman, and child in the city would be turned into stone. This year the lot had fallen on the king's only daughter, who was so beautiful and good that everybody loved her.

'Therefore we wear mourning,' said the old man. 'Therefore we weep and tear our hair and put ashes on our heads.'

'But where *is* the princess?' asked the Knight of the Fish.

'Under the Tree of Ill-Omen, a mile outside the city, waiting for the dragon,' wept the old man.

The Knight of the Fish didn't hesitate a moment. He leaped onto his horse and galloped out of the town. He came to the Tree of Ill-Omen, and found it blasted to a mere white skeleton by the many years of the dragon's fiery breath. And under the tree stood the princess, doing her best to be brave, but shivering from head to foot.

'Oh, fly, fly!' she called out when she saw the knight. 'Fly from this unholy place whilst yet you have time!'

97

'Whilst yet I have time!' cried the knight.

And he swung round and galloped away back to the city.

Now though the princess had meant what she had said, yet to see the knight gallop away like that did add to her bitterness. But in less than no time she saw him come galloping back again, carrying a great mirror balanced against the horse's neck.

'I *am* in time!' he shouted. And he dismounted and leaned the mirror against the tree. 'Now, give me your veil!'

The princess, greatly wondering, unwound the veil from her head and the knight took it and hung it over the face of the mirror.

'When the dragon comes,' said he, 'snatch off the veil. Then quickly step behind the tree, and leave me to do the rest. Do not fear, I shall be ready.' And he went and hid himself and his horse behind some rocks.

Then the earth shook and the air smoked, and out of the smoke came the dragon, breathing fire. When he saw the princess his eyes sparkled, his long spiked tail stood on end and waved to and fro with excitement, and his mouth slavered like the mouth of a hungry dog when it sees a bone. The princess faced him bravely, for though she had no idea how her rescue could come about, yet the Knight of the Fish had given her hope. Looking the dragon full in its hideous face, she put one hand behind her back and snatched the veil from the mirror. Then she stepped behind the tree.

The dragon glared at the mirror, and what did he see? He saw an enemy breathing fire from its mouth, and smoke from its nostrils. He flung up his head and roared with rage. So did the enemy. He lashed his tail, he gnashed his jaws, he rolled his fiery eyes. So did the enemy. The louder he roared, the louder roared the enemy; and opening his jaws to their very widest, and giving such a bellow that the ground shuddered and the branches of the tree groaned and split, he flung himself upon the mirror.

Then the mirror crashed to the ground and broke into hundreds of pieces; and in every piece the dragon saw his writhing enemy. He clawed and bit at his enemy, he swallowed him up, one piece after another. And the pieces of his enemy, as they went down, bit and clawed at his throat and stomach, until he was howling with rage and pain. But that was the end of the dragon, for the knight leaped from behind the rocks and finished him off with his sword.

And when the Knight of the Fish rode back into the city with the princess up before him on his horse, and the head of the dragon trailing behind him on a cord, the bells rang out, the people threw off their mourning, they danced and shouted for joy. They crowded round the knight and the princess, and brought them in triumphal procession to the king's palace. Everyone was shouting that the dragon-slayer must marry the princess.

The king was willing, and the princess was more than willing. And as to the Knight of the Fish, you may be sure that *he* was willing! So the knight and the princess were married. The fountains in the streets flowed with wine; there was a free feast for every man, woman, and child in the city, the feast lasted for seven days, and it was such a time of dancing and singing and merriment as no one could remember in their lives before.

And, after that, the Knight of the Fish, who was now His Royal Highness and the king's heir, went with his bride to live in the palace that had been made ready for them.

The palace was very large and splendid; the knight and the princess went all over it; and the knight looked out from a window and said, 'What castle is that we see in the distance? It looks as if it were made of black marble.'

'That is the Castle of Albatroz,' said the princess. 'Do not let your eyes dwell on it, for it is an evil and enchanted place. Men say that it is the home of the old witch Albatroz, and that there is a curse upon it. Many a brave knight has ridden that way, seeking to destroy the witch. But of all who have ridden that way, not one has come back.'

'But I will ride that way, *and* come back,' thought the knight.

However, he said nothing.

Next morning, when the princess was busy with her maidens, unpacking all the beautiful dresses the king had given her, the knight ordered his horse to be saddled, took his shield, his sword, and his lance, and rode off to the Castle of Albatroz.

It took him many hours to reach that castle; but there he was at last, beneath its great walls that towered above him, black and silent as a starless night. He dismounted and left his dapple horse to graze, knowing that it would come at his whistle. Then he strode up to the castle gate, and gave three loud blasts with his horn.

But no one answered, and no one came. All he heard were the blasts of his horn, loudly echoing from the high black walls.

'Is there no one here?' he shouted. 'Is there no one here alive?'

And back came the hollow voices of the echoes. *No! One! Here! Alive!*

Then the knight lifted his mailed fist and struck as hard as he could on the gate. Five blows echoed like fifty, and before the booming notes had stopped, a small grid in the gate opened, and a hideous old woman peered out at him.

'What do you want?' said the old woman.

'To enter,' said the knight; 'to rest and refresh myself after my long ride. Is there hospitality for travellers here? Is there, or is there not?'

'*Not! Not! Not!*' jeered the echoes.

But the hideous old woman, after peering at the knight for some time, unlocked the gate. 'You are very handsome,' she mumbled. 'You wouldn't do an old woman any harm?'

'*Harm! Harm!*' muttered the echoes. But the knight took no heed of them; and he strode through the gate.

The old woman couldn't take her eyes off him. She seemed to be gloating over his handsome face. She led him into a great hall, and set wine and meat before him. And all the time he was eating, she was leering at him with her horrible mouth, and squinting at him with her horrible eyes.

'Oh, what a beauty he is! What a beauty!' she mumbled. 'Now he has come, he shall never go away again. He shall live with me and be my big handsome husband! You'd like to marry me, wouldn't you, my beauty?'

'*What!*' shouted the knight, so loudly that the hall echoed. '*I* marry *you!* You must be out of your mind! I only came in to rest, and look over the castle. And when I am rested I will go.'

'So you shall, so you shall, my dear,' leered the old woman. 'But the question is – go where?' She gave a screeching laugh, and the echoes screeched with laughter too: '*Ha! ha! Ha! ha! Ha-a-a-ah!*' 'Come along then, you shall see all there is to see, I promise you. And then perhaps you will change your mind and stay.'

'*And stay – and stay – and stay!*' whispered the echoes.

The old woman took the knight all over the castle. She took him upstairs and downstairs and into every room, hopping along on her bony old legs so fast that the knight could scarcely keep pace with her. The castle was full of so many curious things – tapestries where the figures seemed to be moving, and strange old statues that reached out at him, and carved faces that leered at him, and distorting mirrors that made the old woman seem now big as a giant, now tiny as a dwarf, now broad as a balloon, now thin as a thread – so that at last his head began to reel, and he said he had seen enough and would now be going.

'But not until you have seen my greatest treasure,' said the old woman. 'I have kept that to the last; and when you have seen that, I do not know how you will be able to tear yourself away. For it is indeed a treasure beyond price! This way, my beauty. Down these stairs. But I will go first; the stairs are steep and rather dark. Oh yes, you might easily fall!'

The stairs *were* dark, and they *were* steep, and the lower they went the darker and steeper they became. The old woman kept calling to the knight out of the darkness ahead, and he followed her. He began to feel he was a fool for coming, and he stretched out his arm to catch hold of her and bid her return. But the old woman stepped aside into a recess in the wall, and he put his foot on a trap door: the trap door opened under him, and he fell down, down, down into a black pit.

'Ha! ha! ha!' laughed the old woman. '*Now* do you wish you had married Witch Albatroz, you murderer of my dragon son? But revenge is sweet, whether it comes by your life or by your death!'

And she shut the trap door over his groans.

So there we must leave the first Knight of the Fish, and see what the second Knight of the Fish had been doing all this long time. The second knight had wandered here, and wandered there, and met with many an adventure, and performed many a daring deed, though he hadn't come across any dragons. And it so happened that his wanderings brought the second knight to the king's city, just a day or two after the first knight had set out for the castle of Albatroz.

So, on his dapple grey, the second Knight of the Fish cantered up to the city gates, with his armour shining in the sun, and the sign of the white fish gleaming on his shield. To his amazement, as soon as the guards at the gates caught sight of him, they drew themselves up and presented arms; and as he paced slowly along the city streets, the drummers struck up a royal march. Nor was this all: cheering crowds ran at his horse's heels, and, as he drew near the palace, liveried servants came hurrying to tell him that the princess was crying her eyes out for fear that harm had befallen him.

It was then that the second Knight of the Fish realized that he was being mistaken for his brother; and he decided that it would be best to say nothing until he had heard more.

'For it may be that my brother is in peril,' he thought. 'And a blabbing tongue helps nobody.'

So he went into the palace, with everyone bowing before him; and the princess came running down the stairs and flung her arms round him.

'The servants saw you riding away towards that terrible Castle of Albatroz,' she said. 'Did you really go there?'

He looked into her lovely face, all stained with tears. Should he tell her? No, he would not. First let him bring his brother back to her, safe and sound.

'Yes, it seems I went there,' he said.

'And what did you see there, and how did you escape?'

'That I may not tell you,' said he, 'until I have been there once again.'

'Oh no!' she cried. 'Oh no! You have come back alive, isn't that enough?'

Said he, 'Yet I must go, I have work to do there.'

Said she, 'Then at least sleep first. It grows late, and you must be very weary. Come I will bring you to your bed, and we will have our supper sent up to us.'

She held out her hand to him. But he drew back. 'I have sworn never to lie in a bed until I have finished the work that awaits me in the Castle of Albatroz,' he said.

Then the princess left him without a word, puzzled and sad that he was so cold to her.

That evening the second Knight of the Fish lay down to sleep before the fire in the great hall; and early next morning he asked for his horse to be saddled, and rode off to the Castle of Albatroz. The first thing he saw when he drew near the castle was his brother's dapple grey quietly grazing. The two horses greeted each other with whinnies of pleasure; but the knight pressed on, and drew rein before the gate. At the first blast of his horn the old woman opened the gate; but when she saw him she gave a horrible scream, for she thought it was the ghost of the knight she had flung down into the pit.

She turned to run from him, but his sword pierced her. 'Miserable hag,' he cried, 'where is my brother?'

'Oh,' she screamed, 'oh, you have killed me! And if I am going to die, I will tell you nothing. First restore me to health, and then I will tell you.'

'Wretch!' he shouted. 'Can I work miracles?'

'Waste no time in chattering,' she gasped. 'Go into the garden, pluck some flowers of the everlasting plant and some leaves of dragon's blood. Boil them together in a tub, and put me in it. Then I shall recover. But hurry, hurry! Or I shall die, and you will never find your brother!'

He ran to do as the witch had told him. He plucked the flowers and the leaves, and boiled them in a tub; he picked up the hideous dying body of the witch and flung her into the tub. And she came out healed of her wound, but as hideous as ever.

Then, when she had made him swear on his knightly honour that he would not kill her, she told him where his brother was. And he took a torch and went down into the pit, and found his brother lying there without sense or motion. But he brought him up and dipped him into the healing tub, and he sprang out of it, whole and well.

And the two brothers brought up the bodies of all the brave

knights the witch Albatroz had slain, and bathed them in the healing water. And one by one they came back to life. And in another pit they found the bones of the maidens who had been sacrificed to the dragon. And these maidens they also brought back to life.

And when the witch Albatroz saw all the goodly company of knights and maidens gathered outside the castle and free from her spells, she rushed back into the castle, screaming with rage. And as she slammed the door behind her, the castle gave a long sigh, and sank with her into the ground. Where the castle had been there was nothing now but a wide stretch of black earth.

Then, led by the two Knights of the Fish, the whole company of rescued knights and maidens marched off to the king's city. The princess, the wife of the first Knight of the Fish, had been moping over what she imagined was her husband's coldness to her. But now she was smiling again, and wondering how she could have been so stupid as to mistake one brother for the other.

So, when they had all feasted and made merry together, the rescued knights and maidens went back to their various homes: all except one charming little maiden who stayed behind to marry the second Knight of the Fish. And then there was more feasting and more rejoicing. A golden coach, drawn by four prancing piebalds, was sent to bring the parents of the Knights of the Fish to the wedding.

And the story ends, as we know it must end, with everybody living happily ever after.

12 · *Peter*

There was once a merry lad called Peter. And when Peter left school, his father sent him abroad on his travels, that he might learn languages and see something of the world. But that has nothing to do with this story. This story begins when, after three years abroad, Peter comes home again.

Now he must tell his parents of all his adventures. My goodness, how Peter rattled on! His parents could scarcely get in a word; though they might have told him something startling too, if he'd given them half a chance. But their strange news had to wait until the third day, when – did you ever? – a magnificent coach drove up to their front door, a magnificent coach drawn by four coal-black horses, with a driver dressed up so finely that he might have been the king himself, and a liveried lacquey jumping down to rat-tat-tat at the door.

Yes, it was the king's coach, no other; and the lacquey was saying that Peter must come to the king, at once, *at once*.

So into the coach gets Peter. There he sits in solitary state on a red velvet, gold-braided seat, and away goes the coach with the four coal-black horses galloping, galloping, and comes to the king's palace in no time.

'Well, what next?' thinks Peter.

The next is that he's hurried – but oh so politely! – up the palace steps, and in through the great door, and along corridors, this way and that way, until he comes into a mighty big hall, where the king, with his crown on his head and his sceptre in his hand, sits in a golden chair, with the queen sitting in another golden chair at his side.

The king didn't look at all happy, and the queen didn't look at all happy; and as for the hall – well, it looked more than dreary, for it was all hung with black; the windows had black curtains, and except for those two golden chairs, every scrap of furniture in the place was covered with black gauze.

Peter bows, the king beckons, Peter goes up to the golden chair, and waits for the king to speak. The king passes his hand wearily across his brow and says, 'I think you are that Peter who has just come back from three years travelling?'

'Yes, your majesty.'

'Then perhaps you have not heard of the sadness that has over-taken us?'

'No, your majesty, I have been so busy telling my own adventures that – '

'Quite, quite,' says the king; 'so now I must tell you of that sad-ness. But first – one question. Are you a loyal subject? Do you sincerely love us, and are you willing because of that love to risk your life in our service?'

'Oh lordy, lordy,' thinks Peter, 'what's coming now? Risk my life, is it, and I but twenty with so much to look forward to!' But he puts his hand on his heart, makes another low bow, and says, 'I am ready to serve my king to the uttermost.'

'Then listen and feel for us,' said the king. 'You know we have but one child, a daughter, whom the queen and I love with our whole hearts. Ah, ah – three years ago she was so beautiful, so beautiful – she outshone all other maidens as the sun outshines the stars! And so merry she was, with her laughing rosy lips and her roguish sparkling eyes – not a lord, not a knight, not a squire about the court but worshipped the very ground she trod on. Yes, I tell you, the very ground she trod on!'

Here the king made a pause, his voice choked on a sob. And as for the queen, she was quietly weeping.

'Well then,' went on the king, after blowing his nose and clearing his throat, 'it must have been just after you set out on your travels that we celebrated our daughter's fifteenth birthday with an extra great and magnificent banquet. Ah the merry rogue, the merry rogue, how gay she was, how she laughed, and chattered, and teased us all! . . . After the banquet there was to be music and dancing; and with my little princess on my arm I was leading a happy procession of guests into the dance hall, when a carriage came rattling in through the palace gates. . . . But I am getting on too fast. I must tell you, Peter, that I have an aunt, who, from her youth up, has been more wicked than I can say. Indeed truly she is a witch; and she has a daughter as wicked and as ugly as she is herself. So you may think I wasn't pleased when these two scrambled out of the coach and came bursting in upon our birthday party. But I ordered the dining table to be spread once more, and leaving the guests to begin the dancing, my queen and my little daughter and I went back into the dining hall to entertain these unwelcome newcomers.

'Up to that time I had never set eyes on my aunt's daughter; nor did I then see what she was like, for her face was muffled in a veil. But when they sat down to eat, my aunt said, "Now, my daughter, you may take off your veil since we are here alone with our relatives, and there is no young prince or knight present to be struck dumb by your beauty."

'Then the girl laid aside her veil, and – oh heavens! – never have I seen such a monstrous sight! Her nose, immensely long and beak-like, seemed to be trying to enter her mouth; her great mouth stretched from ear to ear, her small green eyes sparkled with demonic malice, and the way she gobbled down her food would have put any self-respecting pig to shame.

'I was quite shocked, and I didn't know what to answer when my witch-aunt, giving me a dig in the ribs with her fork said, "Well now, don't you think my daughter is a hearty handsome girl?"

' "Oh yes, truly hearty, truly hearty," I stuttered.

' "And she is as clever as she is beautiful," said my witch-aunt. "She has so many suitors that it is merely a matter of selecting the most desirable."

'But at that our own dear little daughter, our lovely little princess, burst out laughing.

' "And pray miss, what may *you* be laughing at?" said my witch-aunt.

' "Because, because," laughed our naughty little daughter, "if I were a man I couldn't – no, I really couldn't fancy her, because she is – ha! ha! ha! – so *terribly* ugly!"

' "And what doesn't please you about her, my dear little grand-niece?" said my aunt.

' "Well, the long nose, auntie, the long nose," said my naughty little daughter.

' "Oh, so it's the nose your finding fault with, is it?" said my witch-aunt. "Anything else?"

' "Well, the great mouth, auntie, the great mouth!"

' "So, the mouth," repeated my aunt. "And what else, you clever child?"

' "Ha! ha! ha! The ears auntie, so long and so silly looking. And the little green eyes, auntie – well, don't they make you think of a snake's eyes – a snake when it's in a bad temper? And you, auntie, why you have the very same kind of eyes, so that I should be quite frightened to sit alone in the dark with you!"

'My witch-aunt was still smiling; but never before had I seen – and I hope that never again shall I see – so evil a smile. She rose from the table, gripped our little princess with one horny hand, and passed the other horny hand over the princess's face. "As you have described my daughter's face, so shall your own face be," screamed my aunt. "And so shall your face remain until some gallant youth comes who will marry my daughter, and also perform three tasks that I shall set him."

'Then, having slapped our little princess three times, my aunt took her own daughter by the hand, rushed with her downstairs, out of the palace, and into the waiting coach.

'My queen and I hurried after them, hoping to make the peace. But the coach drove off before we could reach it, so we went back into the palace.

'We found our little daughter sitting alone in the banqueting hall. She had her hands before her face, and she was sobbing. I felt angry with her. I was all set to give her a good scolding. "Well, my girl," I said, "was that the way to treat a guest? *You* a princess, and with no more manners than a street urchin!" And rather roughly, I'm afraid, I took hold of her hands and pulled them away from her face.

'Oh, never shall I forget the horror of that moment! The face that looked up at me was no more like my daughter' face than a hobgoblin is like an angel. Small green eyes squinted, a nose like a pig's snout snuffled, a great slobbering mouth stretched from ear to ear, and the ears themselves were monstrous, long and hairy, like the ears of an ass. No, it couldn't be looked upon, it was unbearable – I seized up a scarf that one of our lady guests had left lying on a chair, and flung the scarf over our poor child's face and head.

'In this guise, and always veiled, she has lived for the past three years. You will remember that the old witch said the spell would only be lifted when some gallant youth married her own daughter, and performed three tasks that she would set him. And though many and many a gallant lad has set out determined to lift the spell, not one of those lads has returned. But I cannot, I will not believe that the witch has destroyed them all! I would rather believe that at sight of her hideous daughter their hearts failed them, and that they fled from her presence into the wide world.

'And now, Peter you can guess why we sent for you. I cannot

command you, but on my knees I, a king, beseech you to undertake this task.'

And there were both king and queen down on their knees before Peter, to his great distress. For no, he did *not* want to marry any witch's ugly daughter, he did *not* want to undertake any horrible tasks, he didn't want to have anything to do with any of it – just when he had returned from his travels, too, and was looking forward to a happy time at home.

'Oh please, oh please don't kneel to me!' he cried. 'I – I – '

At that moment who should come into the room but the veiled princess. And there *she* was also down on her knees before Peter. And though he couldn't see her face, her voice, as she too besought Peter to help her, was like the gentle cooing of a dove, so sweet, so touching, that Peter felt he could deny her nothing. And he said yes, he would go anywhere, he would marry anybody, he would do anything to serve her.

So next morning he set out. The king provided him with a good horse, a purse full of gold, a bottle of wine, and a knapsack filled with delicious food. The sun shone brightly, the birds sang joyously, the flowers in the hedgerows along the way smelled most sweet. And merrily, merrily Peter rode on his way, only pausing once or twice to eat and to let his horse graze. 'After all,' he told himself, 'who would choose to stay pottering about at home, when he could be undertaking heroic deeds in the service of his king and princess?'

But towards evening he came to the entrance of a great forest, and there he was set upon by a band of robbers. He defended himself bravely, but he was one and they were many; they dragged him from his horse, they beat him up, they took away his purse, his horse, the remainder of his food, and his spare clothing. They rode away and left him lying, wounded and bleeding, by the roadside.

'But I still have my life,' thought Peter, 'and that is something to be thankful for!' So he got to his feet and staggered on through the forest, not knowing where to get a night's lodging, or if he got one, how to pay for it.

It was growing dark, too, and our Peter was in a poor way, when he saw, ahead of him, a light glinting through the trees, and staggering on, came to a very small hut. Light shone from the hut's one window, so Peter stepped up to the door and knocked.

The door was opened immediately, and an old, old man, holding a lantern, peered out.

'Who knocks so loud where no one knocks? Who comes this way where no one comes?' said the old, old man.

'A traveller,' said Peter. 'One who has been set upon by robbers, one who has had his horse and his money stolen from him, one who is bruised and battered, one who craves – '

And there he was, tumbled down in a faint on the threshold of the hut. . . .

When he came to himself he was lying on a bed of straw, and the old man was anointing him with a sweet-smelling ointment that took away the pain, and miraculously healed his wounds.

Peter smiled up into the old man's wrinkled face and said, 'I think you must be a magician?'

'Perhaps, perhaps,' said the old man. 'But come, first a bowl of soup, and then you shall tell me your story.'

So, warm, happy, and completely recovered, Peter sat by the old man's fire and told his story, all about the poor little princess and her wicked great aunt, and the great aunt's hideous daughter, and what he was now pledged to do.

And when Peter had finished his story, the old man said, 'It grows late, and now you must sleep. In the morning we will talk together again, for the morning is wiser than the evening.'

On his bed of straw Peter slept soundly, and when he woke next morning, found the old man still sitting in front of the fire, as if he had not stirred all night. But he must have stirred, because the table under the window was laid for breakfast; a pot full of porridge steamed on the hearth, and there were sausages and bacon and eggs ready cooked in a pan.

'Well,' thought Peter, 'let the day bring what it will, it has begun pleasantly!'

And being called to the table by the old man, he ate his fill, and felt strangely contented.

Breakfast over, the old man said, 'My lad, in the silence of night knowledge comes to me. And concerning the three tasks that the witch will set you, here are three gifts that will help you to fulfil those tasks. First a stick, second a golden key, and third a silver whistle. The stick will give motion to that which is struck with it; the key will open every lock. The stick and the key, though somewhat magic, are mild in their working. But I warn you, Peter, that the whistle is so powerful in its action that it will take all your courage to blow it more than once. And yet the hour will come when it must be blown three times if you are to defeat the witch. . . . And now it is high time that you went on your way. Walk straight on through the forest, and you will come out on to a narrow road. Take this road, and after some two miles you will see, on your right, a deep and gloomy dell. In this dell stands a large black house with rows upon rows of small windows. This is the dwelling of the witch-aunt and her ugly daughter. May heaven protect you from them! And so – goodbye!'

Then Peter, having thanked the old man for all his kindness, put the key and the whistle in his pocket, took the stick in his hand, and set out once more.

Walking briskly, he soon came to the end of the forest, and out on to the narrow road: and some two miles along this road found a path that led down into a dell, where among a waste of stunted trees and prickly bushes stood the witch's big black house, with its rows upon rows of little windows, that looked to Peter like so many evil squinting eyes.

'Well, here we begin,' thought Peter, knocking on the house door. 'And heaven only knows how we shall end!'

Knock, knock, knock – and nobody answering. So, since the door was not locked, Peter pushed it open and stepped into a large, bare, and very dirty hall.

'Anybody at home?'

No answer.

'Hey! Hey! Anybody at home?'

No answer.

At the back of the hall was a steep flight of stairs, uncarpeted and festooned with cobwebs. So, after calling several times, and rattatting on the floor with his stick, and still getting no answer, Peter went up the stairs, and came out on to a landing. Behind a door (one of many) on this landing, Peter could hear the muttering of a hoarse voice and the miaowing of a cat. So he knocked on the door.

'What do you want?' screamed the hoarse voice.

'I think – to be anywhere but where I am,' said Peter.

'Well, since you are here, come in,' screamed the voice.

And Peter went in, and found the old witch-aunt feeding a black cat with great lumps of raw meat.

'Another silly fool come to try his hand at disenchanting the princess, I suppose?' said the old witch.

'That's about it,' said Peter. '*And* to marry your daughter, since needs must.'

'I don't know about that,' said the old witch. 'I don't know that she'll fancy such a hobbledehoy. She has her likes and dislikes. And such is her beauty that all the kings in the world are tumbling over each other in their eagerness to make her their queen. . . . Picnotka! Picnotka!' she screamed. 'Come here, my lovely one, and take a look at this young man.'

Then into the room there came clumping the witch's daughter. She was so hideous that Peter simply couldn't bear to look at her. But she looked hard at him, smacked her thick lips and said, 'Give us a kiss, my lovely dovey, because you please me. What – too shy? Never mind, never mind, we'll be married tomorrow, and *then* we'll see which of us is shy!'

'I think,' said Peter, 'I have some tasks to do first?'

'He doesn't want to marry me – think of that!' said the witch's daughter. And she screamed with laughter.

Peter felt angry. He turned to the old witch and said, 'Give me my tasks, if you please. If it will free the princess whom you have enchanted, I am willing to marry anyone, yes, I would marry even the devil's grandmother. But I will *not* be made a fool of!'

'There's a naughty temper for you!' said the old witch. 'But come this way, and I will show you your first task.'

So she got up, and having given the black cat a kick that sent it howling out through the window, she led the way, with Peter and the young witch following, upstairs and downstairs, and along a number of dark passages, until they came into a huge hall, crowded with statues. Or what Peter took to be statues. But were they statues? They looked more like real people, and yet people without life or motion. Some seemed to be about to sit down, some were already sitting, but seemed about to stand up, some seemed to be talking together, some, with bowed head and upraised arms, seemed as if about to run away, and some with open mouths and terror in their eyes, seemed as if voicelessly shouting for help that never came.

'There you are,' said the old witch to Peter. 'Have a good look at them. Maybe you will recognise some friends?'

And to his horror Peter did recognise some of them. For they were his own townsfolk – the gallant lads that had, during the past three years, set out before him in an endeavour to free their princess.

'A real nuisance they are to me,' said the old witch, 'crowding up my best hall; so if you can manage to drive them forth, that shall be your first task. But if you can't manage to drive them forth, then I think you will have to join them. And that would be a pity, wouldn't it, my lad?'

'The stick will give motion to that which is struck with it' – Peter remembered the old man's words. And turning to the figure next to him – a young man who stood with outstretched arms and open mouth as if calling for help – Peter raised the stick and gave that young man a hearty blow on the legs. 'Be off,' he shouted. 'Let me see you run!'

'*Hurrah! Hurrah!*' The young man was shouting, the young man was running, he was dodging in and out among the crowded figures, he was at the door of the hall, and out through the door of the hall, and out of the witch's house, away and away, with never a backward glance.

'*Hurrah! Hurrah!*' Peter was hurrying from one figure to another figure, striking each with his stick, and seeing them come to life and rush away. '*Hurrah! Hurrah!*' The hall echoed with their triumphant shouts. '*Hurrah! Hurrah!*' The whole house was loud with their triumphant shouts. '*Hurrah! Hurrah!*' The sound of their running feet and their triumphant shouting echoed outside through the dreary dell, getting fainter and fainter, until it died away in the distance.

'Task number one duly performed,' said Peter to the old witch. 'And I hope you are pleased?'

The old witch didn't look at all pleased. She was grinding her teeth, and looking as if she would like to murder Peter. But she twisted her mouth into a grin and said, 'Yes, yes, you have done well. But pah! It was but an easy task after all. Come with me now, and you shall have a still easier one. Ho! ho! A *much* easier one!'

So upstairs and downstairs and round and round about, they went again, the old witch leading, Peter and the young witch following, until they came to a great iron door, fast locked with seven padlocks.

'Here is your second task,' said the old witch. 'Open this door for me.'

'That I will gladly do,' said Peter, 'if you have the key handy.'

'*Ha! ha! ha! Ho! ho! ho!*' Old witch and young witch burst into screams of laughter. 'So he wants a key! He wants a key! Well then, let him find a key, for we haven't got one!'

'Perhaps then the stick will manage the business,' thought Peter. And he gave the iron door a blow with the stick.

But the door didn't open.

Again Peter struck the door with the stick.

The door didn't open.

He struck the door a third time.

It didn't open.

'*Ha! ha! ha! Ho! ho! ho!*' The old witch and the young witch were screaming with laughter.

'Your stick may be cleverer than you are,' screeched the young witch. 'But it's not quite clever enough!'

'What now?' thought Peter. 'Is this to be the end of everything?' Then he remembered the gold key that the old wizard had given him. What had the wizard said? 'The key will open every lock.' Peter took the key from his pocket.

Indeed it was a magic key! Peter hadn't even to fit it into the locks. No sooner did the key touch a padlock, than that padlock sprang open; and so with the second padlock, and the third, and the fourth, and the fifth, and the sixth, and the seventh – and when the seventh padlock sprang open, there came such a bang that the whole house trembled, and the iron door fell flat.

'Task number two duly performed,' said Peter.

'So it seems' said the old witch, grinding her teeth again. 'Now come with me.'

Truth to tell, the witch was getting alarmed. Was Peter going to outwit her? Would he be able to perform the third task? And was he going to be fool enough to sacrifice himself even to the extent of marrying her hideous daughter? Ah ha! Such a life they would lead him, she and her daughter! But that was not really what the witch wanted. What she wanted was to revenge herself on the king, the queen, and the princess by keeping the princess under her spell, the impudent little princess who had dared to call her own beloved daughter, her darling Picnotka, ugly.

So now, stepping over the fallen door, she led Peter into her treasure chamber, where gold coins lay in heaps on the floor, and the shelves round the walls were stacked with pearls and rubies and diamonds. Now she was stooped to gather the gold coins from the floor and fill her apron with them; now she was snatching the jewels from their shelves and heaping them on top of the coins in her apron.

'See, Peter, see,' she panted, 'all this wealth I will give you, if only you will refuse to attempt my third task. I can't, I won't allow you to free the princess – the thought is unbearable! What is the princess to you, or you to her, that you should risk your very soul for her? Yes, your very soul, I tell you, for the Lord of Hell is my particular friend.'

But Peter said, 'I don't want your jewels and your coins – put them away.'

'Then I will call up my particular friend,' screamed the witch. 'And as you have a little pipe in your pocket, let us see if *he* will dance to your piping!'

'Very well,' said Peter. 'That shall be my third task.'

And he took out his little pipe and blew on it with all his might. Indeed he scared himself, for the pipe gave out such a loud and powerful note that the very walls trembled, the whole house shuddered, and the old witch screamed out, 'No, no, enough, enough, not another note, not another note, I tell you!'

But Peter blew another note.

Then the walls shook more and more violently; there came a roaring from under the earth; little blue flames darted and flickered up from the floor – and the little blue flames ran round and round in ever widening circles.

'Stop, stop!' screamed the witch.

And 'Stop, stop!' screamed the witch's daughter. And they both tried to snatch the pipe out of Peter's hands. But he held on to it with all his might. Truth to tell he was himself thoroughly frightened, for it seemed to him that at any moment the whole house might come crashing down on to his head. He had to summon all his courage to blow on that pipe for the third time.

But he did blow on it for the third time.

What happened?

The pipe gave out a sound the like of which Peter had never heard in all his life, louder than the loudest thunder: the floor heaved and cracked wide open, and up from a black abyss beneath the floor rose thick clouds of smoke and pillars of flame.

Blinded by the smoke, gasping for breath, choked by the fumes, Peter was lifted from his feet and whirled this way and that. 'This is the end of all things,' he said to himself. And seeking with groping hands for some holdfast, he found none: and so fell to the ground unconscious. . . .

When he came to himself the sun was rising. It was a fresh and beautiful morning, and he was lying on the high ground from which yesterday he had looked down on the dell and on the witch's black house. But where the witch's house had stood was now only a heap of rubble, with here and there a gleam of broken glass, or a smouldering rafter, catching the rays of the sun.

And thinking back on to yesterday's happenings, Peter now remembered that among the smoke and flames rising from that black abyss, there rose also a mighty Being; a mighty Being who, scooping up the old witch under one arm, and scooping up the young witch under his other arm, had sunk with them down again into the abyss. . . . 'And Heaven preserve us from such an end,' thought Peter. 'For surely that mighty Being was the Lord of Hell!'

And so thinking, he got to his feet and went on his way, back to the old hermit's hut in the forest.

'Well, my son,' said the old hermit, 'what news do you bring? Good or bad?'

'I scarcely know, little father,' said Peter. 'With the help of your gifts I succeeded in my tasks. The old witch and the young witch have been carried off to hell, and that is certainly good news. But I did not marry the young witch, and now can never marry her. And so maybe I have not freed the princess?'

'I think there would be great rejoicing in the king's city if you had freed her, Peter?'

'Yes indeed, little father.'

'I think that the whole city would resound with cheers and songs and merry music, Peter?'

'Yes indeed, little father.'

'And perhaps kindly breezes would carry the sound of that rejoicing far and wide, Peter?'

'Yes, little father.'

'Even as far as this forest, Peter?'

'No, no, little father, that is not possible!'

'Not possible? Shut your eyes and listen, Peter.'

So Peter shut his eyes, and the old hermit laid his hand gently on Peter's arm. 'Do you hear anything, Peter?'

'I do – seem to hear – music and singing – and – but so faintly.'

'Listen, Peter, listen.'

Faintly at first, but ever growing louder and louder, Peter heard the sound of fifes and drums, of merry music and the sound of dancing feet, of singing and cheering and happy shouting: 'The spell is broken! Our princess is freed! See where she stands on the palace balcony, smiling down on us! See how beautiful she is, like a lovely rose, like a shining star, like the sun in heaven! Heaven's blessing on our beautiful princess, and on the gallant lad who has freed her from the witch's curse!'

'Go to her, Peter,' said the old hermit.

And he gave Peter a gentle push. . . .

Where was Peter now? He was back in the king's city, surrounded by a great throng of cheering people. He was being led up to the king's palace, and there was the king himself, taking him by the hand and bringing him into the palace, and along the corridors, and this way and that way, and into the mighty big hall, which, when last Peter saw it, had been hung with black, but which was now gay with coloured tapestries, and bright with flowers. And here, lovelier than any flower, was the princess herself, running to fling her arms round his neck, and calling him her dear, *dearest* Peter, and kissing him again and again.

And the queen too, the happy queen was there, welcoming Peter as 'her own dear son'. And Peter's father and mother were there, bursting with pride, you're sure. And now king, queen, Peter's parents, Peter and the princess all go out on to the balcony, where Peter must stand hand in hand with the princess, and bow again and again to the cheering crowd below.

So, without more ado, we come to the end of the story. For as soon as might be, Peter married the princess, to live with her in happiness ever after.

13 · Catrinella, come up higher!

Once upon a time there was a beautiful orphan girl called Catrinella who took service with a farmer's wife.

Every morning, in company with several of the village girls, she went to collect firewood in a forest at the foot of a great mountain.

Now at the top of the mountain lived the Frost Demon, Morez, so it was said, though no one had ever ventured to go up and find out. And if Morez did live at the top of the mountain he never came down into the forest, so the girls felt quite safe in gathering wood there. But on the very first day that Catrinella joined the other girls a strange thing happened! There came a loud voice calling from the mountain and echoing through the forest. And the voice was calling: *'Catrinella, come up higher! Catrinella, Catrinella, come up higher!'*

My word, but the girls were frightened! They left their bundles of wood lying and scampered for home.

Well, they got scolded for coming back empty-handed. And next morning they all went again into the forest. At first everything was quiet. Then came the voice: *'Catrinella! Catrinella! Come up higher!'*

And again the girls scampered for home.

So it went on day after day – every morning that loud voice from the top of the mountain calling Catrinella. But, as nothing else happened, and as the owner of the voice never appeared to trouble them, the girls got used to its calling, and went boldly to the forest and gathered their sticks and brought them home. They even teased Catrinella about the voice. 'Hark, there's your lover calling you, Catrinella,' they would say. 'Only fancy, the demon Morez has fallen in love with you! Well, no wonder, you're pretty enough for anything!' So they laughed and joked.

But Catrinella was puzzled. *Why* should a voice be calling her?

And the voice sometimes sounded so desperate, as if the one who called was in great trouble. Was someone suffering up there on the mountain top, and calling and calling for help that never came? Certainly it couldn't be Morez the Frost Demon – *he* could very well look after himself! Who then? 'I can't bear it,' thought Catrinella, 'if the voice calls again I shall have to go up!'

Next morning Catrinella went as usual with the other girls to the forest. Everything was peaceful: the girls rambled here, rambled there, broke off small dead branches to fill their sacks, laughed and joked. 'Your lover's lost his voice this morning, Catrinella,' they said. 'What will you do if he never finds it again?'

'I think – I should be very glad,' said Catrinella.

'Oh, oh, do you hear that, Catrinella's lover?' laughed the girls. 'She doesn't want you – what a shame!'

And then suddenly they were all silent, for there was the voice calling again – calling more loudly, more desperately than ever before.

'Catrinella, come up higher! Catrinella, come up higher!'

Catrinella flung down her sack and said, 'I'm going up.'

'Oh no, no, Catrinella, don't, don't!' The girls were really frightened now. 'He'll kill you, the demon Morez will kill you! Come home quickly!'

But Catrinella turned from them, and went her way through the forest and up the mountain.

Up, up, up, and all the time the voice calling from above her, 'Catrinella, Catrinella, come up higher!' She was climbing all day, and came at sunset to a frozen plateau on the mountain top. Now there was no higher to go, and the voice was silent. Catrinella looked about her, and saw the arched entrance to a great cave. She peered into the cave. What did she see? She saw a company of handsome young fellows seated on horseback, some with bows and arrows, some with spears, but all turned to ice. And at the frozen horses' feet lay many beautiful hounds, and they also were ice.

The coldness of that cave almost took Catrinella's breath away. She was going out again, when the same voice called her, only now very quietly, 'Catrinella! Catrinella!'

'Who – who calls me?' faltered Catrinella.

'It is I, prince Ilya,' said one of the frozen riders. 'I cannot move, I cannot come to you; but I can still use my voice. Oh, if you have any pity in your heart, redeem my companions and myself from this frozen death!'

'I will help you if I can,' said Catrinella, whose teeth were chattering. 'But what can I do?'

Then prince Ilya told a sad story. 'I was hunting with my companions,' he said, 'on the other side of this mountain, when we gave chase to a great golden-horned stag. The stag fled up the mountain, and we followed; but when we came to the top of the mountain the stag gave a leap and disappeared into the clouds. Then there fell from the clouds a great storm of snow, and we all rode into this cave for shelter. But in the cave sat Morez, the Frost Demon, sparkling with rage. "How dare you trespass here?" he roared; and clapping his blue hands he turned us all to ice. "And ice you shall remain," said he, "for a hundred times a hundred years. No sun shall have power to warm you, no fire shall have power to melt you, for I am stronger than the sun, and more powerful than any fire, except the fire that glows in the heart of the great diamond that is hidden in the Palace of Shifting Rooms in the Kingdom of the Uttermost East, where the sun rises to warm the earth. None may lay hold of that diamond but a maiden who has no guile. And where in the world is the maiden who will risk her life on that venture?" he screamed, and went away in a swirl of icy wind, leaving us all frozen, as you see.

'The days passed, the nights passed, but one night into my frozen brain there came a dream. The dream was of you, Catrinella. I saw you bringing the diamond that should set us free, and so I called you. Oh Catrinella, if you will do my comrades and myself this great service, I will bow myself at your feet, and offer you all that I have and am!'

The poor prince! So young, so handsome, so pitifully enchanted! Catrinella felt she would do anything for him. 'But – but how shall I find the way to this Palace of Shifting Rooms?' she asked.

'That I do not know,' said the prince sadly. 'Yes, I see, what I ask of you is impossible.'

'Impossible! Rubbish!' buzzed a voice.

And flying into the cave came a bumble bee.

'*I* know the way, and I can show it,' buzzed the bumble bee. 'But it's a long, long way. I might drop dead of fatigue before we got there. You would have to carry me now and then.'

'I would gladly carry you,' said Catrinella.

'Then come along quickly,' said the bumble bee. 'It's too cold to loiter here. My wings are almost turned to ice already!'

So Catrinella and the bumble bee set out. But to tell of all their journeying would take a lifetime. Down the other side of the mountain they went, and up and down over other mountains, and through forests where wolves howled and lions roared, and across deserts where Catrinella had to shut her eyes against the whirling sand, and along the banks of rushing, roaring rivers. Catrinella's shoes were in tatters before the end of that journey, and she would have starved to death, had not the bee shown her where to find honey and edible roots.

And ever they travelled towards the sun rising, and so came at last into the kingdom of the Uttermost East. And there before them rose a stone mountain. And at the foot of this mountain was a gaping rocky cleft.

'Now,' said the bumble bee, 'you must go down into that cleft. I can't come with you any farther, because being underground doesn't agree with my health. But I will wait for you here. You will find a path which leads into the middle of the mountain. Follow the path until you come to a stone wall barring your way. Take off one of your tattered shoes and strike the wall with all your might. Then it will fall apart, and behind it you will see the Palace of Shifting Rooms. Somewhere in that palace the Great Diamond is hidden – the Great Diamond with the heart of Glowing Fire. But I do not know where it is hidden. You must seek until you find.'

Then the bee flew to settle himself on a thistle, which was the only plant that grew in that desolate place. And Catrinella went down into the cleft under the mountain.

Down and down and down, along a steep and stony path with great rocks towering on either side of her: at times stumbling and almost falling in a twilight that grew ever dimmer; at times having to feel her way among the crowding boulders – down and down and down. Until at last the path ended in a high stone wall, and she could go no farther.

Then Catrinella, remembering the bee's instructions, took off one of her tattered shoes and struck the wall with all her might. *Crash!* The wall fell down, and Catrinella stepped over the fallen stones into a fair green meadow.

In the meadow a dappled horse was grazing. When he saw Catrinella he flung up his head and galloped towards her, whinnying with delight. But Catrinella only spared a moment to give him a kiss on his soft nose, and a pat on his glossy neck: for beyond the meadow rose the glimmering walls of a palace, the Palace of Shifting Rooms. And now Catrinella, with all her weariness forgotten, was running like a hare across the meadow and up a flight of glass steps, and in at a door which opened at a thrust of her hand and shut silently behind her.

Where was she now? In a great room with walls of glass. At the farther end of this room was an open door, through which she could see more glass rooms with open doors, and more glass rooms and more, one glass room behind another, one glass door behind another, and getting smaller and smaller in the distance until they appeared no bigger than her hand, and smaller yet, until lost to sight.

And what a wonder – there were no windows and no lamps, and yet it was all as light as a midsummer morning; and on the glassy floor Catrinella could see her own image reflected: standing as she stood, and moving as she moved. So from the first glass room she went through the open door into a second glass room, and through the open door of this second glass room into a third, and into a fourth and a fifth and a sixth. But they were all empty. And as she went the walls were continually shifting: sometimes receding so far on either side that she could scarcely see them; sometimes moving up so close on either side that it was all she could do to squeeze herself through them.

And she began to be very afraid.

'But I have not come all this way just to turn back now,' she said to herself. And on she went and on. But everywhere was emptiness. And where in this vast emptiness could she find the great diamond she had come so far to seek?

On and on and on. Now she came into a huge room with gold pillars standing in rows down either side of it, and an arched glass roof. There was no door at the farther end of this room, so it must be the last room in the palace. And still she hadn't found the diamond! Well, she would look carefully behind every pillar, and then go back the way she had come, and search each room again.

So about and about that huge room she went, pausing often to admire the gold pillars, which were embossed with patterns of flowers and birds and trailing plants. And so, in searching here, and searching there, she happened to look behind her. And oh, now she was really terrified. For the door by which she had come into the room had vanished, and behind her was only a solid wall of glass! Yes, she was caught like a fly in a bottle – no way forward, no way back!

'Oh, what can I do?'

She put her hands before her face and wept.

'What's the matter here? What's the matter?' shrilled a tiny voice. And there, standing on his hind legs at her feet, was a little white mouse. 'A great girl like you, blubbering like a baby!' said the little white mouse. 'You ought to be ashamed! And what are you doing here, I should like to know?'

Well, even the company of a little white mouse was comforting, and Catrinella sat down on the glassy floor and told the mouse all about everything. And when she had finished her story, the mouse said, 'You're a brave girl, and I like you. But I can't have you crying – I don't like that! And dear me, what a fuss about nothing! I know where the diamond is, and if you'll stop crying, and dry your eyes, and stand on your feet, I'll show you.'

So then Catrinella did stop crying, and the mouse brought her to stand behind one of the gold pillars.

'Now,' said he, 'you see that pattern of a willow tree on the pillar? And you see the image of a kingfisher standing on one of the branches? And you see that the kingfisher's got a swollen throat, as if he had just swallowed a big fish? Well, he *has* swallowed something, but it isn't a fish. Reach up, give him a slap, and he'll spit out what he's swallowed.'

So Catrinella stood on tiptoe, reached up her hand to the golden pillar, and gave the kingfisher a slap. What happened? The kingfisher opened his beak, wide, wide, wide: and down at Catrinella's feet fell a crystal box. And there, in the crystal box, on a cushion of red velvet, was a diamond, so big, so sparkling, so burning bright, that it might have been a fragment of the very sun itself.

'Pick up the box,' said the mouse. 'But hold on to it tightly and stand steady on your feet if you can, because there's going to be a whirligig in here!'

So Catrinella picked up the crystal box – and, my word, there *was* a whirligig! The whole palace seemed to be turning round and round; Catrinella was lifted off her feet, tossed here, tossed there, whilst invisible hands plucked at her, trying to snatch away the box. But she clung to it with all her might, and the next moment she was standing on the grassy meadow outside the palace with the crystal box still in her hands, the little white mouse at her feet, and the dappled horse rubbing his nose against her cheek, and saying, 'I know a short cut to the mountain of Morez, I'll carry you there in no time!'

Then Catrinella, with the precious crystal box under her arm, and the little white mouse perched on her shoulder, got on to the horse's back, and off he went like the wind. Which way he went Catrinella couldn't tell; but no sooner had he left the stone mountain behind, than there was the bee flying up from the thistle in which he had been sleeping, and perching himself on Catrinella's other shoulder. And so, galloping, galloping the dappled horse came in a very short time to the foot of the Mountain of Morez, and never pausing, galloped up the mountain and came to a stand outside the cave on the mountain top.

'Catrinella, Catrinella,' called the familiar voice from inside the cave. 'Have you really come again?'

'Yes, I have come,' cried Catrinella, sliding off the back of the dappled horse. 'I have been to the Palace of Shifting Rooms in the

Kingdom of the Uttermost East, and *I've got the diamond*, the diamond with the glowing fire in its heart!'

'Well then, into the cave with you,' said the white mouse, 'and open the box. But do it with your eyes shut, lest the blaze of the diamond blind you.'

So Catrinella went into the cave, shut her eyes, and opened the box. And well for her that she did shut her eyes, for the diamond lit up the whole cave with a flaming light that was indeed almost blinding. And in that light the ice melted from the walls, and the hounds and the horses and the riders were warmed into life. Out of the cave they rode shouting and singing, with the horses neighing and the hounds barking at the horses' feet. And Catrinella followed them, leaving the diamond to blaze in its box on the cave floor, for there was no getting near it to pick it up again.

And outside the cave prince Ilya leaped from his horse and knelt at Catrinella's feet.

'Catrinella,' he said, 'I have no words to thank you. I can but offer you all that I have and am. If you will come to my kingdom with me and be my wife, I will love and cherish you to the end of my days.'

'Yes, I will come,' said Catrinella.

Then away they all rode, down the mountain, the whole company of them, and the bee and the mouse went with them, perched on Catrinella's shoulders. And all along the way flowers sprang up to welcome them, and the birds sang for very joy. So, in a short time, or a long time, they came to prince Ilya's capital city, where the townsfolk ran out into the streets laughing and cheering. Never in this world was there a happier home-coming, or a happier wedding than the wedding of prince Ilya and Catrinella.

As to the demon Morez: when he came back to his mountain top he found it in flames. Nor with all his puffing and blowing and his wicked magic could he put out those flames. So he fled far away to some place or another place – who knows to what place?

And left the mountain burning to this day.